SLAM DUNK!

As Reggie Dupree dribbled midcourt, Patriot star center Brian Davis ran along the base line, then cut sharply toward the free-throw line. Quiller center Garrett stayed with him.

"Dupree!" Brian shouted, raising his right hand for a pass. Reggie looked the other way, then zipped a chest pass to Brian. He caught the ball and turned to face Garrett.

Davis got him off balance with a quick head fake, then dribbled between his own legs and drove for the hoop. Leaping high, he slammed the ball through the basket.

Other Books in the **HOOPS** series:

TOURNEY FEVER

Kirk Marshall

BALLANTINE BOOKS ● NEW YORK

Special thanks to Steve Clark.

RLI: $\dfrac{\text{VL: 6 \& up}}{\text{IL: 6 \& up}}$

Produced by the Jeffrey Weiss Group, Inc.
96 Morton Street
New York, New York 10014

Library of Congress Catalog-Card-Number: 89-90950

ISBN 0-345-35912-7

Manufactured in the United States of America

First Edition: September 1989

For the Lincoln kids—Jennifer, Jonathan, and Heather.

TOURNEY FEVER

ONE

"Davis!" shouted Reggie Dupree. Jefferson's five-foot-ten guard raised his right hand for a pass.

Brian Davis, the Patriots' junior center, jumped as high as he could and ripped a rebound away from a leaping Northport Hawks player. Landing on the court with his elbows out, Davis faced Dupree, who stood near the midcourt line.

"Fast break!" Tom Ford, Jefferson's head coach, shouted from the bench.

Brian whipped an overhead pass to Reggie, who started dribbling downcourt.

"I got the right wing," said LaMont Jackson, the Patriots' senior captain. The six-two black forward raced down the right side of the court beside Dupree.

"I got the left," shouted Terry Hanson, Jefferson's playmaker. The redheaded senior turned and formed a three-man fast break with Reggie and LaMont.

Clarence Reed, the Patriots' power forward, quickly nudged Brian and pointed downcourt.

"Be the trailer, homeboy," yelled the muscular black senior, adjusting the protective eye goggles he wore.

Brian nodded and sprinted downcourt. He pumped his long legs as fast as he could and caught up to his teammates just as Reggie stopped at the free-throw line.

Three Northport Hawks defenders had run downcourt and stood near the hoop, closely guarding Jackson, Hanson, and Dupree.

"Trailer!" Brian shouted, approaching the foul lane.

Reggie turned and flipped a scoop pass to Brian, who cut toward the basket.

The Hawk defender who'd been guarding La-Mont switched over to Brian, leaving the Patriots' captain open for a pass.

Brian faked the Northport player out of position and zipped a behind-the-back pass to LaMont, near the hoop. The six-two forward laid the ball in and gave Jefferson the lead 2–0.

The packed Jefferson High gym exploded with cheers.

"*LaMont Jackson, he's our man!*" shouted the Patriots' cheerleaders. "*Go, LaMont, go!*"

"Nice pass, homeboy," LaMont told Brian as they ran downcourt to play defense.

Clarence Reed bashed forearms with Brian. The forearm bash had replaced high-fives for the Patriots as their team salute.

"Way to run the break, Davis," Reed said.

"Yeah, and pass the ball to us seniors," Terry

Hanson said, smiling and hitting forearms with Brian.

The Patriots' Friday-night game against Northport was not only the last pre-tournament game of the season, but it was also their last home game. And at Indianapolis's Jefferson High, as at many Indiana high schools, that meant it was time to honor the senior players for the last time.

LaMont, Reed, Hanson, reserve center Jeff Burgess, and third-string center Nick Vanos had been presented to the three thousand fans before the game. They received a standing ovation.

"Keep the passes coming, Davis," Reed added with a big grin. "Man, I can't remember Brian passin' up a shot before."

"Don't knock him," Reggie said as he started to play defense. "Dude's averaging thirty points a game."

"Yeah, but now he's gotta share some of his hoops with us poor seniors," Terry added with a laugh.

Brian smiled and prepared to play defense. As the Northport Hawks ran toward him to set up their offense, he quickly recalled the scouting report the Patriots' coaches had discussed before the game.

"Sean McCartney, Northport's six-six white forward, is their best player," Coach Ford had told the Patriots in the locker room. "Likes to shoot from the corners."

"Dude can rebound, too," Coach Mel Williams, the heavyset black assistant coach, had added, "so block him out."

"Northport's next best player is five-eight black play maker Leroy Sampson," Coach Ford continued, glancing down at the notes on his clipboard. "He's first and shoots three-pointers."

"What about their center?" Brian had asked.

"The kid's name is Dale Ruffing," Coach Ford said.

"He's nothing, Davis," Tony Zarella had said, rubbing the black stubble on his face. The bushy-haired junior guard always seemed to need a shave.

"Ruffing's a skinny dude who can barely jump," Reggie had said with a smile. "You oughta eat him up, bro."

Reggie and Tony bashed forearms with Brian. They had been his closest buddies since last summer, when he moved with his mom from the small country town of Paintville, Indiana, to Indianapolis. They taught him about inner-city hoops and made his transfer to big Jefferson High easier.

"Ruffing goes for fakes," Coach Ford had added, looking at Brian, "so use your moves on offense."

Brian snapped back into the game as the Northport Hawks began their downcourt. He found the skinny center Dale Ruffing and stuck with him.

"Pick up your men," LaMont shouted, pointing at the Hawk players.

But before Brian and the other Patriots began guarding closely, Reggie stole the ball from Northport's five-eight playmaker, Leroy Sampson, and headed downcourt.

"Fill the fast-break lanes!" LaMont shouted.

Brian turned away from Ruffing and ran down the left side of the floor. Terry took the lane on the right side, and Reggie dribbled to the free-throw line and stopped.

Sean McCartney, Northport's star forward, was

the only defender between the three Patriots and the basket.

Reggie looked at Terry on the right, then threw a blind chest pass to Brian on the left. McCartney seemed to expect the pass to Davis, and slid over to block the way to the hoop.

Out of the corner of his eye, Brian spotted Terry waving his hand under the basket. He faked once with the ball, then shot an underhand pass to Terry, who made an unguarded lay-up shot.

The Jefferson rooters stood and cheered. The patriots' pep band drummer pounded away. The score was 4–0.

"Nice pass, Davis," Terry said as they ran down-court to play defense.

"Man, we oughta have Senior Night more often," Reggie said.

"Ain't that the truth," Clarence said, bashing forearms with Brian. "Don't forget, Davis, I'm a senior, too."

For the rest of the first quarter, the Northport Hawks played lame ball. They threw bad passes, traveled while dribbling, and shot before they were ready. The Patriots held a tight defense, stopping McCartney from shooting in corners and stealing the ball whenever they had the chance.

On offense, Reggie and Terry looked for Brian coming off picks set by Clarence and LaMont. Brian cut around the picks four times, caught sharp passes, and swished jumpers over Dale Ruffing's outstretched arms. LaMont used shake-and-bake fakes to get Sean McCartney off balance, then drove to the basket for three lay-ups. McCartney fouled him twice, then just before the period ended slapped LaMont again for his third foul, and was taken from the game.

At the end of the first quarter, Jefferson led Northport 28–12. LaMont, scored twelve points, mostly on quick passes from Davis. Brian added nine, as well as four rebounds.

"We're killing these jerks!" Cisco Vega said as Brian and the other starters returned to the bench between quarters.

"McCartney's in foul trouble," Coach Ford shouted to the Patriots over the pep band's loud music. "I doubt we'll see him much more this half. That'll hurt their offense."

"But keep working on defense," Coach Williams added.

The Jefferson cheerleaders finished a tumbling routine on the court, and the second quarter was about to begin. Brian and four of the starters opened the period on the bench. Only Clarence returned to the floor, this time playing center for Brian.

"Let's go, subs!" Brian shouted as he towled off beside Reggie and LaMont. "Make 'em work, Reed."

"We gonna need you bench dudes in the tournament," Reggie added, "so show us something."

Besides Clarence at center, Coach Ford sent sophomore forward George Ross and junior forward Brad Cunningham onto the court. Alvin Woolridge and Tony Zarella went in as guards.

Except for Sean McCartney, the Hawks sent their starters back onto the court. After tossing in the ball to begin the period, Northport quickly scored on a driving lay-up by Leroy Sampson. The

Hawks' speedy playmaker flew past Tony, who seemed nailed to the court.

"Move your feet, Zarella," LaMont shouted from the bench.

"Help each other," Brain added, yelling over the crowd noise. "You can beat these guys."

But the Northport starters, obviously happy to be playing against Jefferson's subs, poured it on. During the next four minutes, Leroy Sampson swished two shots from beyond the three-point arc, stole the ball three times, and drove to the basket for two unguarded lay-ups against the Patriots' reserves. Even Dale Ruffing swished a jump shot and grabbed two rebounds against Ross and Cunningham.

With the score Jefferson 32 and Northport 26, Coach Ford turned to Brian and the other starters.

"Get in there," said the coach in a disgusted voice. "Our subs are stinking up the gym."

"Man, we gonna need some good play from our bench in the tournament," Reggie told Brian as they walked back onto the court. The subs trudged past them to the bench.

"No way the starters can play the whole game," Brian said. "It's been a long season, and I'm tired already."

"I'm glad to see you dudes," Reed said, wiping his goggles with his jersey. "Let's kick some butts."

"Work the plays," LaMont shouted as the Patriots prepared to toss in the ball. "They're playing man to man."

Reed accepted the ball from the ref, then slapped it as a signal for the Patriots to cut into position. LaMont turned away from Reed, set a solid pick behind Ruffing, and braced himself for contact as Brian cut past him. It was an out-of-bounds play they'd used often.

Brian was open for Reed's lob pass and slam-dunked the ball through the hoop. The Jefferson rooters cheered.

"That's more like it," Reed said, bashing fore-arms with Brian and LaMont.

"Now let's hold 'em," LaMont shouted.

With the score Jefferson 34 and Northport 26, the Hawks were more confident than they'd been in the first quarter.

Running downcourt to play defense on Ruffing, Brian saw Leroy Sampson fire a length-of-the-court pass toward Sean McCartney, who was running just ahead of Ruffing. Brian leaped, inter-cepted the pass, and tapped the ball to Reggie, who started back toward the Patriots' basket.

"Dupree!" shouted Reed, twenty feet from the basket.

Reggie whipped a long chest pass to Clarence, who dribbled once and dunked the ball through the hoop.

The Patriots' fans stood and cheered, as did the Jefferson subs. The score was now Jefferson 36 and Northport 26.

The Hawks again inbounded the ball to Leroy Sampson, who dribbled quickly over the midcourt line. Brian found Ruffing standing near the base line with his right hand raised for a pass. Sampson looked one way, then snapped a chest pass to Ruffing.

A step behind the skinny Northport center, Brian leaped and reached over Ruffing, trying to block the shot. But as Ruffing laid the ball in the hoop, Brian slapped him across the arm for a foul.

"Nice try, homeboy," Reed told Brian.

"Time your jump better," LaMont said.

Ruffing missed his free throw, and Brian hauled in his fifth rebound of the half. He passed the ball to Terry at midcourt, and the Patriots set up their half-court offense.

For the rest of the half, Jefferson and Northport played about even. Sean McCartney swished two long jumpers from the right corner for the Hawks and Leroy Sampson made another three-pointer. For the Patriots, LaMont drove easily around McCartney and the other Northport forwards for eight more points. Davis noticed Ruffing was playing back, so he swished three three-point jump shots just before the quarter ended.

At half time, the score was Jefferson 44 and Northport 32. LaMont had scored twenty points, while Brian added seventeen.

"We gotta work harder on defense," Coach Ford told Brian and the other Patriots in the locker room during the break. "Northport's getting too many open shots."

"One loss in next week's tournament," Coach Williams added in his deep voice, "and we're out, so let's practice stopping these easy hoops."

The starters returned to the floor just as the Jefferson pep band finished a fight song.

"We're making these dudes look good," Reggie said, nodding at the Northport starters.

"Yeah, time to act serious," Clarence said, pulling his goggles over his eyes.

"And play tough D like coach said," LaMont reminded his teammates, clapping his hands.

Northport tossed the ball inbounds to Leroy Sampson. Reggie hounded Sampson into passing wildly to McCartney, and LaMont intercepted the ball.

"Fast break!" shouted Hanson, racing downcourt.

Brian sprinted down the left side of the court and formed a three-man break with Terry and Reggie. LaMont became the trailer and Clarence stayed back on defense.

Sean McCartney ran back to play defense, but it was three against one.

Dupree passed the ball to Hanson on the right side of the basket, and McCartney leaped to guard him. Terry tossed a high-arching lob pass to Brian.

Brian caught the ball with one hand, took two giant steps toward the hoop, and slammed the ball through the basket so hard that the metal support poles hanging from the ceiling rocked back and forth.

The Jefferson fans exploded with a loud cheer.

"Nice slam, homeboy," Reed said, bashing forearms with Brian as they ran back to play defense.

"That'll show these guys who's gonna win," Terry added, clapping his hands.

For most of the third quarter, the Patriots controlled the game. LaMont scored twice on twisting lay-ups. Brian swished two more three-point jump shots, tapped in a miss by LaMont, and drove past Dale Ruffing as though the Hawks center were in slow motion.

By the time the starters left the game and the Patriots' subs took over, the score was Jefferson 64 and Northport 37. The only bad part of Brian's play during the quarter had been his attempts at shot blocking. He'd failed once and was faked out of position twice by McCartney.

For the rest of the third quarter, Brian and the

other starters watched the subs struggle to maintain the Patriots' big lead. Jeff Burgess, a senior who also was a football star, used his size to muscle Dale Ruffing out of position.

"Push that skinny dude around, Burgess," Reggie shouted from the bench.

"Seniors always play tough," Terry added, bashing forearms with fellow seniors LaMont and Clarence.

When Northport cut the patriots' lead to ten points early in the fourth quarter, Coach Ford sent Brian and the starters back into the game. Brian shot over and around Ruffing twice, and LaMont drove around McCartney for two lay-ups. With the lead back to sixteen points, Coach Ford took Brian and the Seniors from the game for the last time.

LaMont, Clarence, and Terry got a standing ovation.

"Way to go, seniors," Coach Williams said, bashing forearms with the three sweaty players.

"We're gonna miss you guys next year," Tony said to the seniors as he toweled off on the bench.

Brian had just settled back to watch the subs when his replacement at center, Jeff Burgess, leaped for a rebound under the Hawks' basket. The big football player landed awkwardly on the court, twisting his right knee, and fell to the floor.

The gym, which had been filled with happy cheers, suddenly grew quiet and tense. The coaches ran to Jeff's side.

Coach Ford placed an air-filled splint around Jeff's right knee until an emergency medical unit arrived and wheeled him on a stretcher to an ambulance in the parking lot.

The Jefferson rooters gave Burgess a round of applause. But what began as a happy night for the seniors finished on a sad note for Brian and his teammates.

The Patriots won the game 94–80, and their pre-tournament record was now sixteen wins and four losses. The victory would put Jefferson back among the state's top twenty teams.

But in the locker room, Brian and the other Patriots were thinking about Jeff Burgess as the team dressed quietly.

Brian spoke briefly about the upcoming tournament with a sportswriter who'd just interviewed Coach Ford. Then, hoping to catch up to Reggie and Tony, Brian stepped out into the February chill and almost knocked into a man waiting near the door of the poorly lit locker room.

"Excuse me," Brian said, looking down at the short middle-aged man. The guy was neatly dressed in an expensive topcoat and wore wire-rimmed glasses. He smiled up at Brian.

"That's okay. Hey, you're Davis, right? My name is Mo Gernert," the man said, shaking Brian's hand. His grip was firm and his voice pleasant. "I've been a Jefferson Patriots fan for a long time, and I just want to say you're the best center they've had in a long time. Lots of luck in the tournament."

"Uh . . . thanks," Brian said awkwardly. Being the star center for the Patriots, he often shook hands with fans after games. But there was something weird about this guy.

"I'll be watching you," Mo Gernert said, smiling. Brian just nodded and walked away, hoping he'd catch up with his friends at Burger Heaven.

TWO

"Man, I can't believe Burgess is out for the season," Reggie said. He shot a jumper at the hoop nailed to the garage behind Brian's aunt's house.

"Coach Ford said Jeff tore up his knee real bad," Tony Zarella added. "They're gonna operate tomorrow."

"You guys see how bad his knee was twisted?" Cisco Vega said, shooting at the hoop.

"Tough luck for Burgess," Brian said, lofting a long jumper toward the basket.

"Well, Burgess was a senior," Tony said. "At least he did it on Senior Night."

The Patriots tossed their basketballs at Tony.

It was noon on Sunday following the victory over Northport, and Brian and his teammates were waiting for Coach Ford to stop by with some news. The Indiana High School Basketball Association was pairing teams for the state tourney that morning. The coach promised to tell Brian and his friends whom the Patriots were going to play first in the sectional tournament.

"Hard to believe it's tourney time already," Tony said, dribbling around the driveway.

"Yeah, the season went fast," Cisco said.

"Seems like it was only yesterday we were suffering through the coach's drills," Brian said, swishing another long jump shot.

"Leave it to homeboy to bring up Coach Ford's torture sessions," Reggie said, smiling.

"Yeah, just when I was getting psyched about the tournament," Tony said, playfully punching Brian in the arm.

"Some states don't even have all-school tournaments," dark-haired Cisco said, shooting a jumper at the hoop.

"Say what?" Reggie said.

"That's right," Brian said, tracking down his bouncing ball. "Only Indiana and Kentucky let all the schools play no matter what their record was during the season. There was an article about it in *Sports Illustrated*."

"Man, that's the only way to do a tournament," Reggie said. "Everybody gets a chance to win it."

"Yeah, that's the way to do a tournament," Tony agreed, bashing forearms with Reggie.

"Too bad we gotta do it without Burgess," Cisco said, shooting a jumper.

"We still got Nick Vanos," Brian said.

"Man, you kiddin', Davis?" Reggie said, spinning his ball on his right index finger. "Dude's out of it."

"Yeah, Nick never comes to practice, Tony added. "I hear he's drunk half the time."

"Like father, like son," Cisco said, referring to Nick's alcoholic dad.

Brian thought about his own dad, a recovering alcoholic living in Oklahoma, but didn't say anything.

"That's all we need," Reggie said, passing his ball around his back to his other hand. "Burgess is down with a busted knee and Vanos can't keep it together."

"No sweat," Brian said, smiling. "I'm working on my shot blocking. After I slap back the shots of all the other centers, I'm gonna rest on defense."

"Man, if Ruffing can score on you, anybody can," Reggie said, laughing.

"Hey, Davis, the dude's challenging you," Tony said.

"Okay, Dupree, show me your moves," Brian said, getting into a defensive crouch.

"Let's see some shake-and-bake, Reg," Cisco said.

"Come on, Davis, how about a basketball sandwich for Dupree?" Tony added with a laugh.

"Dupree's in trouble now."

"No way," Reggie said, dribbling toward Brian and the hoop on the garage.

Faking several times with his head and shoulders, Reggie drove to the basket. Brian reached up to block the shot, but missed and swatted air instead. Reggie laid the ball in the hoop, then turned and smiled at Brian.

"Gotcha," Reggie said, pointing at Brian.

"Lucky," Brian said. "Let's do it again."

"Eat him up, Dupree," Cisco shouted with a laugh.

Reggie faked and feinted again, but this time Brian didn't leap out of position. When Reggie

shot his lay-up, Brian reached up and slapped the
ball as hard as he could.

It smacked into the garage door, shattering a
window.

Shards of glass rained onto the driveway.

"I think we're in trouble."

"Uh, see you guys later," Cisco said, edging
toward the street leading to his house.

The back door of the house opened, and Brian's
mom, a small, pretty woman, looked out at them.

"Brian?" she asked. She glanced at Cisco, who
stopped and smiled at her.

"What was that crash?" Brian's Aunt Margaret
asked as she stepped up behind his mom. She
looked like his mom, only taller and with graying
hair. "Sounded like glass."

"We . . . we had an accident," Brian said.

"Not another garage window," his mom said.
"They cost twenty dollars to fix."

"No problem," Aunt Margaret said, wiping her
hands on the apron around her waist. She smiled
at Brian and his teammates. "What's a busted
window once in a while so long as the Patriots win
the tournament?"

"All right!" Cisco said, smiling again. "Davis,
your aunt's something else."

"Don't worry, Aunt Meg, we'll clean up the
mess, won't we, guys?"

"Yeah, Brian'll get on it," Tony said, shooting at
the basket.

Everyone laughed, then his mom and aunt went
back in the house. Brian swept away the broken
glass.

"It's getting warmer," Brian said, "so maybe we

oughta go to the park after supper and get us a full-court game."

"Sounds good," Reggie said, shooting over Brian, who was sweeping up the last of the glass.

"Yeah, and the park doesn't have any windows for Davis to break," Tony said, laughing.

An hour later, Coach Ford walked down the driveway.

The four Patriots stopped playing.

"Who'd we draw for the first game, Coach?" Tony asked.

"What day do we play?" Cisco said.

"I think we lucked out, guys," the coach said, looking at a slip of paper. "We play Boorman at eight o'clock next Tuesday night. If we beat 'em, then we play the winner of the Northport-Baptist game on Friday night."

"Coach, Boorman's no problem, " Reggie said.

"Yeah, they're a bunch of wimps," Tony added. "Can't have more than a hundred guys in the whole school."

"Some of those Catholic schools are tough," Cisco said, "but Boorman ain't one of 'em."

"Just remember what we always tell you guys," Coach Ford said, "if you think a team's going to be a pushover—"

"—then they'll probably beat you," Brian said, finishing the coach's sentence for him.

"Yeah, but us against Boorman?" Tony said. "Coach, you might as well mail in the official stats now." He bashed forearms with Cisco, Reggie, and Brian.

"Who else is in our sectional?" Brian asked.

"Oakridge, Eastside, Pine Grove, and St. Francis," the coach said. "We beat 'em all during the season."

"Man, who we gonna play in the regional?" Reggie said boastfully.

"Let's win the Sectional first," Coach Ford said.

"I like our chances," Brian said, "but I also remember what happened this season when we were too cocky."

"Like against South Central and Zellinger," Coach Ford added, mentioning two games the Patriots should have won.

"Maybe," Reggie said, "but I'm still looking for us to be playing in the Regional."

"Too bad we gotta wait till next week to play Boorman," Cisco said. "I wanna go at 'em now."

"Yeah, but then you'd miss a full week of tough practices," Coach Ford said with a smile as he walked toward his parked car. "See you at school tomorrow."

"Thanks a lot, Coach," Tony said sarcastically.

After supper that evening, the four Patriot teammates walked to a nearby park for a pick-up game.

"Man, look at all the dudes playing ball," Reggie said, pointing at the four asphalt courts surrounded by a battered chain-link fence. Floodlights lit the full-court games.

"We oughta find a good game," Tony said.

"Yeah, us Patriots can't be seen playing against just anybody," Cisco added with a smile.

Brian and his friends each carried a ball with JEFFERSON HIGH stenciled on it. Coach Ford gave one to each varsity player to carry wherever he went, even in school.

"I want to work on my shot blocking," Brian

said as he followed the others through a hole in the fence.

"Let's find some little guys so Davis can slap the ball back in their faces," Tony said, laughing.

Within five minutes, the four Patriot players chose a young white kid to join them and started a full-court game against five older black kids from another part of town.

The game was no contest. The Patriots were awesome.

"Dupree!" Brian shouted just after the game began, his right hand raised.

Reggie tricky-dribbled around one of the out-of-position black kids on the other team and whipped a hook pass to Brian in the right corner. He stood twenty feet from the basket.

"Come on, Davis, show me your stuff," taunted a tall black kid who knew Brian's reputation as a shooter.

Brian up-faked once with the ball and the kid leaped at him, hoping to block the shot. Brian ducked under the airborne defender, dribbled twice, and slam-dunked the ball through the rusty rim.

"Way to move, Davis," Tony said, bashing forearms.

Before the other team crossed the midcourt line, Reggie lashed out with his right hand and stripped the ball from one of their inexperienced guards. He dribbled downcourt.

Brian raced beside Reggie in a two-on-one fast break.

The two Patriots passed the ball back and forth until the lone defender nearly fell backward. Then

Brian zipped a behind-the-back pass to Reggie, who laid the ball in.

The other team finally managed to dribble across the half-court line and set up its offense. One of the opposing guards broke free from slow-footed Tony, caught a pass, and drove to the basket.

Brian was ready to block the shot back into the kid's face.

Switching away from the man he was guarding, Brian leaped high. But the driving guard stopped in his tracks and faked up with the ball, and faked Davis out of his socks.

The guard passed between Brian's legs to a teammate, who missed the lay-up. Cisco rebounded the missed shot.

"Great move, shot blocker," Tony said, kidding Brian.

"Guess I need some more practice," Brian said.

"You're better at smashing windows," Cisco added playfully.

Twenty minutes later, the Patriots scored their fifteenth basket and won the pickup game 15–6.

"Lookin' good, Davis," said a voice behind Brian.

Brian turned and looked at a tall black guy who had his hand extended. The broad-faced man, who was smartly dressed and in his mid-twenties, stood about six foot five, and had the look of a former basketball player.

"Name's Mickey Wright," the guy said, shaking hands with Brian. Wright's hands were huge.

"Hey, aren't you the guy who played at Indiana University?" Tony asked, stepping over to Brian and Wright.

"The same Mickey Wright dude who dropped outta college after only one year?" Reggie said, joining the group.

"The one and only," Wright said, forcing a smile.

"Yeah, I remember," Cisco said. "You were Indiana's top scorer your freshman year."

"What happened, man?" Reggie asked.

"You know, sometimes things don't work out," was all Wright said. Then he looked at Brian again. "I dropped by to see my main man, Davis."

"You mean the shot blocker?" Tony said, chuckling.

"I mean one of the best high school players in Indiana," Wright said, winking at Brian.

"This guy knows talent when he sees it," Brian said, pointing at Wright and smiling at his teammates.

"Sure I do," Wright said, "and I know a big dude like Davis gotta choose the right college basketball program. Someplace where he can play right away and be a star."

"Davis?" Cisco said, shaking his head. "A star?"

"Gimme a break, Vega," Brian said.

"I know from experience," Wright continued, "what kind of pressure a dude like Davis is under. You know, TV and everybody else build things up. But I got a way to cut through all that crap. A way to make sure Davis gets his break."

"What's that?" Brian asked, putting on his jacket in the evening chill. Mickey Wright was saying things he wanted to hear.

Wright looked around, then pulled Brian away.

"Sorry, fellas," Wright said, smiling at the other Patriots, "but I gotta talk to my man in private."

"Sure, don't mind us scrubs," Tony said.

"We ain't goin' nowhere," Reggie said.

Brian and Wright stopped near the chain-link fence.

"I know a guy with lots of connections in big-time college basketball programs," Wright said, looking around nervously. He lowered his voice. "Dude's name is Mo Gernert."

"So, what is he, an agent?" Brian asked, wondering what he was getting into. The man's name sounded familiar. He felt a nervous pang in his stomach. "I . . . I can't get involved with him if he is."

Wright shook his head and patted Brian on the shoulder. "Relax, man," he said. "Gernert's been a fan of Jefferson High hoops for years. He likes helping good players get the best deal in college. Makes him feel important."

"Does he know Coach Ford?"

"Sure, Mo knows everybody," Wright said. "But he likes to work in private, you know, without the coaches gettin' involved. Dude likes to do things on his own."

Brian looked at his teammates, then figured he owed it to himself to help his future as a college player.

"So," Wright continued, "don't tell nothing to your coach until after you talk with Mo. See what the dude can do for you. You ain't got nothin' to lose."

"I guess it'll be okay," Brian said.

Wright smiled and patted Brian's shoulder again.

"Remember, keep this quiet for a while," Wright said. He nodded at Brian's friends. "Don't say nothin' to those dudes, neither. Gernert'll be in touch soon."

After Mickey Wright walked out of the park and slipped into the passenger side of a late-model car, Brain rejoined his teammates near the court.

"So?" Tony asked as they all walked toward home.

Brian hesitated.

"Come on, Davis. What's going on?" Reggie asked.

"We talked about college ball, that's all," Brian said finally. "I'll probably never see Wright again."

"Weird, Davis, the whole thing's weird," Tony said.

"Just don't tell this to anybody," Brian added.

"How come?" Cisco said.

"'Cause I promised," Brian said, "and because it ain't worth making trouble over, anyway."

Brian saw the strange looks on his friends' faces as they glanced up at him. Then they all walked out of the park in silence.

THREE

Tourney fever had hit Jefferson High. The school's hallways, cafeteria, and classrooms were decorated with red-white-and-blue streamers. Posters showing the Patriots capturing a Boorman Bearcat hung everywhere, and the cheerleaders practiced their yells between classes, getting everybody even more psyched for the sectional tourney.

Even Mr. Rhodes, the principal, was acting like a crazy freshman. He poked his head into the gym while the Patriots were finishing their laps and shouted, "Go, Patriots, beat Boorman!"

"Man, the school's going bananas," Clarence said.

"Okay, guys, listen up! We've only got a week to get ready for the tournament," Coach Ford shouted as Monday afternoon's practice began, "so work hard. All the other teams are, you can count on it."

"And start thinking about the Boorman Bearcats," Coach Williams added in his baritone voice.

"Man, more like the Boorman Pussycats," Reggie said, laughing as he ran laps with Brian and the other Patriots.

"What a joke," Terry Hanson added.

"Maybe," LaMont said, huffing and puffing as he led the team around the court, "but we can't play anybody else until we beat those dudes. Think about that, guys."

Brian was glad to think about something else besides Mickey Wright and Mo Gernert. He'd spent Sunday night tossing and turning in bed while thoughts of his weird meeting in the park kept him awake.

"Hey, where's Vanos?" Tony asked nobody in particular after the team finished their laps and took a water break.

"Dude's probably strung out on booze somewhere," Reggie said, wiping his mouth with the back of his hand.

"Nick was out today," Terry said as the players walked back onto the court. "The kid next to me in English said he's got the flu or something."

"Yeah, right," Tony said, tipping his hand back as if drinking from a bottle.

"Maybe he'll straighten out," Brian said. "With Burgess out, we'll need him for the tourney."

After practice, Brian stayed on the court with Coach Williams. They were alone in the gym.

"You've improved a lot this season, Davis," the heavyset black assistant said, "but your shot blocking still needs work."

"Is there a trick to it?" Brian asked as they walked under one of the main baskets.

"Jumping helps. And timing," Coach Williams said, smiling.

Brian nodded.

"Most dudes think they gotta block the ball into the bleachers. And they try to block every shot."

"That's wrong?"

"Sure, 'cause if you can't block a shot, then try to make the shooter change the way he shoots," Coach Williams said, tossing a ball to Brian. "Go ahead, shoot a lay-up the way you usually do."

Brian dribbled to the hoop and made a lay-up off the backboard.

"Do it again, but this time watch what happens when you got a hand in your face."

Brian shot another lay-up, but this time Coach Williams leaped and blocked his face. Brian tried to avoid the coach's hand and missed the lay-up.

"See," Coach Williams said, huffing and puffing from the sudden effort, "I made you change your shot. Same thing goes for jump shots."

"Sorta psyching out the shooter," Brian said.

"Right," the coach said, bashing forearms with Brian.

They changed positions. Brian leaped and smashed the coach's shot off the court.

"Great block, but keep the ball in play," Coach Williams said as Brian retrieved the ball. "Tap it to a teammate and start a fast break toward your own hoop."

Brian caught on quickly and after an hour of practice, he had his moves down cold.

When Nick didn't show up again on Tuesday,

Brian, Reggie, and Tony decided to visit him at home after practice.

"Dude's not thinking about his teammates," Reggie said as they approached the Vanoses' white two-story house.

"Even if Nick's a jerk," Tony added, "we need him for the tournament. After all, it's the sectional."

Brian led the way up the creaking front steps and onto a large porch. He pressed the doorbell and a minute later Nick opened the door and squinted at them. He was dressed in rumpled clothes and looked like he'd been sleeping. His eyes were bloodshot.

"Remember us?" Tony asked, smiling awkwardly.

"Hey, man," Reggie said, "we missed you at practice."

Brian watched as Nick licked his lips and looked behind him into the house. Then he stepped onto the porch.

"I . . . I been sick," Nick said, his voice hoarse.

When Nick spoke, Brian and the others smelled the alcohol on his breath.

"Cut the crap, man," Reggie said, waving his hand in front of his nose. "You smell like a six-pack."

"You been drunk as a skunk the past two days, ain't that right, Nick?" Tony snapped.

Brian saw Nick's dark face twist into a scowl.

"So what?" he shouted, looking at them. "It's none of your damn business."

"Man, you're a drunk who don't care about nobody," Reggie said. "Same as your old man."

Nick's eyes flashed with anger. He stepped

toward Reggie, his fists balled. Brian and Tony stopped him.

"Cool it, Nick," Brian said, straining to hold back the six-four reserve center. "We came here 'cause the team needs you."

"Yeah, with Burgess out, we need a center to back up Davis for the tourney," Tony added, holding on to Nick's arms.

Tony's words hung in the air for a moment.

Brian and Tony released Vanos. Nick shook his head and took a deep breath. "Guys, you're right, and I'm sorry I missed practice."

"So's Davis," Reggie said. "Dude's been doing double duty on all the drills for centers."

All four of them laughed, then Nick nodded.

"I'll be there tomorrow," he said, licking his lips again. He nodded back toward the house. "It's just that things are kinda tough around here with my dad, you know?"

Brian nodded. "Yeah, don't worry about it," he said. "Just get your butt back to practice."

"And lay off the booze," Reggie said, leaning closer to Nick and winking.

"Yeah, or Coach Mel'll sweat it out of you with his famous drills," Tony added, chuckling.

Nick entered the house, and Brian and his teammates headed for home.

"What do you think:" Brian asked.

"Nick's known for making promises," Tony said.

"Yeah, but not for keeping 'em," Reggie added.

"Hey, we're back in the top-twenty ratings," Reggie announced as he read the morning sports section.

He was walking along a sidewalk with Brian and Tony.

"What's our ranking?" Brian asked.

"Number seventeen in the state," Tony said, running his finger down the list of high school basketball ratings.

"Dudes makin' that list are smart," Reggie said.

"Yeah, and they're picking us to win our sectional," Tony added. "Says here we oughta win the regional, too."

"That's cool," Reggie said, spinning the ball he was carrying on his right index finger.

It was Saturday morning and the three teammates were heading for the Jefferson High gym to watch the final games of the neighborhood Biddy Basketball League.

"Look at the pep-rally stuff," Reggie said, pointing at some nearby stores and office buildings.

Brian looked up from Tony's sports page and saw red-white-and-blue streamers flowing from some parked delivery trucks. He also saw hand-painted signs on several storefront windows that read Go Patriots! or Good Luck, Jefferson!

"It's the fever," Tony said as they approached the local Seven-Eleven store. "Our fans get behind us every year when tournament time rolls around."

A car passed and the driver honked his horn.

"Good luck in the tourney, guys!" the driver yelled as he sped by.

Brian and his two teammates waved, then walked into the Seven-Eleven store.

"You're right, Zarella," Brian said, "our fans are psyched."

Inside the store, they saw a wide banner hanging from the ceiling that read Go Patriots! in big red-white-and-blue letters. Mr. Riley, the manager, was smiling.

"Boys, I got a deal for you," said the balding store owner. "You win the sectional and the Cokes and candy bars are on the house next week."

"Might as well pay up now, Mr. Riley," Tony said, tearing off the wrapper from a Milky Way. "We're gonna win."

Mr. Riley frowned and extended his hand. "Well, son, deal begins *after* you win."

Brian and Reggie laughed as Tony paid up and they left the store.

Shrill screams filled the near-empty gym and hurt Brian's ears. Two games were taking place at once on the small courts that ran across the main court the varsity used.

Brian saw seven-and eight-year-old players running up and down the courts. What they lacked in skill they made up for in enthusiasm. Parents stood around both courts and applauded the wild action in front of them.

"These are the championship games for the little kids," Tony said. "The game for the twelve-year-olds is gonna start pretty soon. That's the one to watch."

"Some fast dudes are gonna play," Reggie added. "a couple of 'em can even dunk the ball."

The little kids finished playing, and as the Patriots signed autographs for some fans who recognized them, the bigger kids trotted onto one of the courts for their game.

The twelve-year-olds were warming up when

Tony nudged Brian and pointed at the gym's main entrance.

"It's Vanos," Tony said.

Brian looked up. "What's Nick doing here?"

"His brother plays on one of the twelve-year-olds' teams," Tony said.

"Man, he looks drunk," Reggie said.

Brian stared at the Patriots' reserve center and saw him wobble as he walked toward the courts.

"Nick said he'd stop drinking," Brian said. He watched Vanos bump into some parents.

"I got a bad feeling about this," Tony said. "We better do something before it's too late."

"It's already too late," Brian said, pointing at the far court. "Look at him now."

The three teammates watched as Nick took a swig from a beer bottle, then hauled a teenager from a chair.

"Let's go," Brian said, running across the court and through the warm-up drill of one of the teams.

"Nick's a jerk," Reggie said, following Brian.

"Yeah, but we gotta save him," Brian said. He jumped over some chairs along the sideline. "He's our teammate."

Brian reached Nick just as he was about to punch the teenager he'd pulled from the chair.

"Whoa, Nick," Brian said, grabbing the reserve center's arms, "take it easy." Reggie and Tony stopped the teenager.

"Let me go," Nick said in a slurred voice. "I wanna watch the game and this guy won't let me."

Brian looked around and saw that everybody in the gym was watching them. Even the teams had stopped warming up.

"Come on, Nick, let's go home," Brian said quietly.

"No, I wanna watch the game," Nick shouted.

"Man, there's only one way to do this," Reggie said, smiling at some nearby parents and shoving Nick toward the door. "Get the Dude's other arm, Zarella."

The bottle in Nick's hand fell and shattered on the court, but soon the three Patriots had him out of the gym and stumbling down the steps to the sidewalk. Twenty minutes later, Brian and his two friends set Nick on an old couch on his front porch. Vanos was sleeping like a baby.

"Man, we gonna hear about this at school on Monday," Reggie said. "So's Nick, if he's sober by then."

They shut the porch door and walked toward home.

"Man, the whole school knows what happened to Nick," Reggie told Brian between classes on Monday. "The dude's being treated like a criminal."

"I heard Mr. Rhodes got two dozen phone calls today from parents who were at the Biddy games," Tony added. "I wouldn't want to be in Vanos's shoes about now."

At lunch, Brian heard more bad news.

"Vanos left school after fourth period," Tony said.

"Say what?" Reggie asked.

"Nick's heard so much crap from the kids, I figure he decided enough was enough and split," Tony said. "He's been laughed at in all his classes."

At practice Monday afternoon, as Brian and his

ten remaining teammates warmed up, Nick stum-
bled into the gym. He was drunk.

"I don't need you guys," Nick shouted.

The players stopped shooting and stared at him.

Coaches Ford and Williams walked toward
Nick.

"Man, the dude's in big trouble now," Reggie
said.

Brian watched as Coach Ford grabbed Nick's
arm.

"Vanos," the coach said in a firm but understanding voice, "this is the last straw. You're off
the team."

"Lemme go . . ." Nick shouted, trying to tear
free. He was drunker than Brian had ever seen
him.

The coaches finally calmed the six-four center
and led him toward the main office. In the gym,
the players remained stunned, and stared after
Nick.

"Hey, guys, we got a tournament game tomorrow," LaMont said, clapping his hands. "Let's
practice."

Brian and the other Patriots started warming up
again, but their mood was gloomy.

"Well, homeboy," Clarence told Brian as they
fired jump shots, "now it's official. We ain't got a
backup center."

"Yeah, better get used to playing the whole
game, Davis," Terry said.

Coach Williams returned to the gym and the
players ran twenty-five laps around the court.
When they finished, Coach Ford walked through
the locker-room door with a tall, skinny kid who
seemed scared and nervous.

"Eddie Logan?" Tony said. "He's just a freshman."

"Dude's a B-team player," Reggie added.

Coach Ford gathered the team at the midcourt circle.

"You guys know Eddie," the young head coach said, indicating the blushing six-five kid beside him. "We need a reserve center for the tourney and Eddie's it. Help him learn our plays and get him ready for the sectional."

"It's tough that Eddie joined us so late," Coach Williams added. "Davis, teach him to play varsity center."

Brian nodded, and the Patriots began their practice.

"Let's beat those Boorman Bearcats," LaMont shouted, trying to get the team psyched. "We can do it."

"Yeah, all right!" yelled several players.

The team's spirit was back. Brian and his teammates worked for two hours preparing for their opening game of the tournament. He taught Eddie all the plays involving centers, and the freshman learned fast.

"Way to work, Eddie," Terry shouted, bashing forearms with the newest Patriot. "Just watch Davis do it."

"Yeah, the dude's ugly but he knows what he's doing," Reggie added with a smile.

The players laughed, and soon they'd forgotten about Nick Vanos and the incident at the start of practice.

"Okay, we're ready," Coach Ford said finally. "Get a good night's sleep and be ready to win tomorrow."

"Hey," LaMont said, stopping the players as they headed for the locker room. The six-two black captain smiled. "It ain't right to let Logan join the team without doing the drill." LaMont winked at Zarella.

"Jackson's right," Tony said, rubbing his stubbled face thoughtfully. Then he brightened. "Logan's got to go one on one against Davis for ten baskets."

"Sounds cool," Reggie said, "and when he loses—I mean *if* he loses—the dude's gotta carry the ball bags on the bus during the tournament." Reggie laughed at his own idea.

The coaches chuckled, and soon Brian and Logan stood with a ball at one of the main baskets.

"Eat him up, Logan," Tony shouted with a laugh.

"Don't hurt the dude, homeboy," Reed said.

Brian looked at Eddie, who seemed to be all arms and legs. The freckle-faced freshman caught Brian's pass.

"You go first," Brian said, crouching into a defensive position. "Let's see what you got."

Eddie dribbled a few times, backed into Brian, then tried a turnaround jump shot.

Brian blocked the shot and grabbed the ball.

"Nice block," Coach Williams shouted to Brian. "Remember what we worked on."

The other Patriots whooped and hollered on the sidelines. Coach Ford watched and smiled.

Brian dribbled near the free-throw line, faked once with his head, and drove past Eddie as if the surprised kid were nailed to the floor. Brian slam-dunked the ball.

Eddie was nervous for the first five minutes. Then the six-five rookie gained some confidence and played better. Brian swished five shots in a row, but Eddie finally scored on a nifty up-fake and a jump hook shot.

"Way to move," Davis told the freshman, who smiled.

Ten minutes later, Brian scored the final basket and won the game 10–3.

"Looks like we got us a backup center, after all," Tony said as the Patriots ran to the locker room.

FOUR

"Man, this looks like a game," Reggie said, looking at the packed bleachers in the Jefferson High gym.

"Yeah, what a pep rally," Tony added. "I've never seen everybody so psyched."

The players and coaches stood at midcourt while the pep band played a fight song.

It was Tuesday afternoon, the day of the first tournament game, and classes were called off early so the school could give the Patriots a rousing show of support. The gym walls were decorated with posters and streamers, and the air was full of red-white-and-blue confetti.

"Look, it's your mom and aunt," Tony told Brian, pointing at a spot in the bleachers. "Seems like half the neighborhood's here, too."

Brian waved at his mom and Aunt Margaret, who were two of the Patriots' best fans.

The band finished playing and the cheerleaders led the crowd in some spirited yells. Then Lori

Harper, a pretty blonde cheerleader from Brian's homeroom, ran past and patted him on the arm. Brian felt embarrassed and blushed.

"We're gonna win, Brian!" Lori shouted, clapping.

Mr. Rhodes spoke into a microphone at midcourt and the fans grew silent.

"What a great crowd," shouted the small, grayhaired principal, "and what a great team!" He gestured at the Patriots.

The crowd cheered and applauded. The pep band's drummer pounded away until Mr. Rhodes raised his hand to quiet him.

"I want to see all of you at the Butler fieldhouse tonight," the principal said, pointing at the fans, "so we can root our guys on to victory over Boorman."

"*Beat Boorman! Beat Boorman!*" shouted the crowd. Tony leaned closer to Brian.

"Mr. Rhodes really gets into it," he said.

"Dude's gonna blow a fuse," Reggie added.

"Now," said Mr. Rhodes as the cheers died down, "here's the best coach in the state of Indiana, Tom Ford."

Brian and the other Patriots led the cheers for their coach, who stepped up to the mike.

"With your help, Jefferson's going all the way this year!" Coach Ford said.

The fans rose and cheered, and the band played.

"Here are *your* Jefferson High Patriots," the coach continued, gesturing at Brian and the players.

For the next few minutes Coach Ford introduced the team. As he called each name, the player walked out into the middle of the court and stood in line. Brian felt embarrassed when he got the loudest applause. After the team returned to their places, Mr. Rhodes took the mike and thanked everybody for coming. The pep band played the fight song until the last fan had left. It was the biggest pep rally in the history of Jefferson High.

"This place is like a dungeon," Terry said, looking around the ancient Butler fieldhouse locker room.

"Yeah, all that's missing are bars," Tony added.

"Man, it's cold enough to be a dungeon," Clarence said, pulling on his blue uniform. For this first game, the Patriots were the visiting team, and Boorman wore white jerseys.

"It's okay," Brian said, smiling at Reed. "I'll warm up the fieldhouse with my hot shooting."

The players booed and tossed towels at Brian.

Ten thousand screaming fans were already watching the first game of the evening between Northport and Baptist High, and the Patriots were getting impatient. The tourney pressue was building.

LaMont must have realized Eddie Logan was more nervous than anybody.

"Don't let these dudes bother you, Eddie," said the team's captain, nodding at the players. "They're always crazy."

The six-five freshman center smiled sheepishly. A few minutes later, the coaches arrived to discuss the Boorman Bearcats' scouting report.

"What do you guys remember about Boorman?"

Coach Ford asked, looking at the scouting report they had talked about at yesterday's practice.

"James Robinson," Reggie said, nodding. "He's a six-three black dude who's quick. Drives down the lane a lot."

"He's all yours, Dupree," Coach Ford said.

"Shut him down," Terry said, bashing forearms.

"Make Robinson take long shots," Coach Williams added. Keep him away from the hoop and you'll stop him."

"What about Boorman's other players?" Coach Ford said.

"Their next best player is a six-four white guy named Lance Petty," LaMont said. "Dude likes to shoot jumpers."

"Your man, Jackson. Make him drive to the hoop," Coach Ford said. "And block him away from the boards."

"Their center's a six-seven black guy," Brian said, remembering the scouting report. "Name's Norman Gaines. He's kinda awkward and doesn't rebound much."

"Make him shoot from the outside," Coach Williams reminded Brian. He smiled. "Dude couldn't hit the side of your old barn back in Paintville."

Coach Williams laughed deeply, and the team joined in.

A loud cheer from the crowd in the fieldhouse above them was followed by a knock on the locker room door.

"Jefferson, the first game's over," said one of the tournament's organizers. "You got twenty-five minutes before you play."

"How bad did Northport beat Baptist?" Reggie yelled through the closed door.

"They didn't," came the reply. "Baptist upset 'em by two points."

The Patriots exchanged surprised glances.

"That shows you what can happen," Coach Williams said, stroking his goatee. "Northport's done for the season and it could happen to us if we're not careful."

"No way, Coach," Terry shouted. "We're awesome."

"That's cool," Clarence added, clapping.

"Yeah, let's show 'em who's the best team in the sectional," Tony said, standing along with the others.

"And in the state," Reggie said, bashing forearms with everybody.

They huddled around the coaches and thrust in their hands.

"Okay, guys, let's win 'em one game at a time," Coach Ford said. "Ready! One, two, three!"

"Let's go!" shouted the Patriots, raising their hands together and heading for the door.

Brian and his teammates buttoned their blue warm-ups and ran up the long ramp leading from the basement locker rooms to the huge fieldhouse. They trotted onto the brightly lit court to shoot lay-ups just as three thousand or so Jefferson High rooters stood and cheered wildly.

Only one pep band was allowed to play each night during the tourney, and for this opening session the Eastside High band was playing a loud rock song. The cheerleaders from Jefferson and Boorman were leaping along the sidelines.

Brian looked around the old arena and saw

rows and rows of fans all the way up to the rafters. Dozen of sportswriters, TV announcers, and radio people filled the seats known as press row.

"Man, we ain't had so many people at a game before," Reggie told Brian as they waited in the lay-up line.

"They're here to watch us beat Boorman," Brian said, his stomach churning nervously.

The Boorman Bearcats, led by six-foot-three James Robinson, warmed up at the other basket. One thousand of their fans, including dozens of priests and nuns, tried to cheer more loudly than the Patriots' rooters, and the noise echoed in the rafters.

After twenty minutes of jump shots and lay-ups, Brian heard the buzzer calling both teams to their benches. The lineups were introduced, and then Brian and the usual Jefferson starters walked to the midcourt jump-ball circle and shook hands with Robinson and the Boorman starting five.

The cheering sections for both schools went wild.

Brian wiped the sweat from his palms and prepared to jump against Norman Gaines.

Cameras flashed and the cheerleaders yelled.

The official tossed up the ball and the state tournament began for the Patriots. Brian reached as high as he could and tapped the ball to Terry, who dribbled downcourt. Brian ran after him.

"They're playing zone!" LaMont shouted above the noise in the fieldhouse. "Set up the offense!"

Brian saw the Bearcats were in a two-three formation, with Robinson out front and Gaines near the hoop.

"Work the plays," Coach Ford shouted from the bench. "Look for good shots."

The players on both teams were nervous, and Brian took advantage of Boorman's jitters. He cut to the middle of the zone defense, raised his right hand, and caught a sharp pass from Terry.

Brian turned, pump-faked once, and swished a jumper.

The Patriots' rooters exploded with a cheer, and Brian's teammates bashed forearms with him.

"Play defense," LaMont said, pointing at the Bearcats, who now were running toward their basket.

"Pick up your men," Coach Ford yelled from the bench.

Brian found Gaines and stuck with him. But Reggie couldn't do the same with Robinson.

The speedy Boorman guard flashed some shake-and-bake dribbling moves near midcourt, left Reggie three steps behind him, and raced to the hoop for an easy lay-up.

The score was now 2–2. The Boorman fans cheered loudly.

"Man, the dude's quick," Reggie said as the Patriots ran downcourt for offense.

"Stay with him or we're hurtin'," Brian said.

The Patriots worked the ball against Boorman's two-three zone defense. Reggie zipped a pass to Terry, who passed to LaMont, who snapped a chest pass to Brian under the hoop. The Bearcats closed in on him.

"Shoot, man," Gaines told Brian, taunting him.

Brian up-faked once, twice, and then shot a soft jumper into the basket. Gaines smacked him on the arm and was whistled for a foul. Brian swished his free throw, and the Patriots led 5–2 after only two minutes of play.

"Pick up Robinson," LaMont shouted, pointing as the Bearcats' guard dribbled downcourt again.

"I got him," Reggie said, but came in too tight and the refs whistled Reggie for a shoving foul.

"Man, I didn't touch the dude," Reggie complained.

"Forget it and get on Robinson," LaMont said.

The Bearcats inbounded the ball and passed it to Robinson again. Reggie stuck with him for a while, but then the slick-dribbling guard stopped and started a few times near the free-throw line and breezed past Reggie to the hoop.

Brian watched as Reggie caught up late and fouled Robinson as he was laying the ball in.

The Boorman fans stood and cheered. Reggie swore under his breath.

Robinson made his free throw and the score was tied, 5–5.

The rest of the first quarter saw the Patriots feeding Brian for jumpers over Boorman's two-three zone or LaMont for drives around it. But Reggie and Terry missed a few long jump shots, and Clarence was fouled twice but missed his free throws. And for Boorman, James Robinson scored fourteen points on drives past Reggie and Terry, and the quarter ended tied, 20–20.

The Bearcats' fans went wild, but Brian and the other Patriot players trudged off the court and slumped onto their bench.

"Dupree, try and force Robinson toward Davis," Coach Ford shouted over the cheers and music in the fieldhouse.

"That'll give you a chance to use your shot

blocking," Coach Williams yelled at Brian. "Remember, you don't have to make a block all the time. Just get the dude to change his shot."

Both teams began the second quarter with the same lineups, and Boorman inbounded the ball to Robinson.

"Stop that dude," Clarence shouted at Reggie.

Reggie stayed with Robinson, but ten seconds after the quarter started, he reached in for a steal and slapped Robinson's arms for his third foul. The Jefferson fans groaned and Coach Ford sent Alvin Woolridge into the game.

"I'll stop him, Reg," Alvin said as Dupree walked to the bench with his head down.

"Pick up your men," LaMont said as Boorman inbounded the ball again. "Look for a double team."

Robinson caught the inbounds pass and dribbled over midcourt, where suddenly LaMont jumped away from Lance Petty and formed a double team with Alvin. The move surprised Robinson, and he was whistled for traveling.

The Boorman fans yelled a the refs.

"Way to go!" shouted the Patriots subs.

"Gotcha that time," Alvin said into Robinson's face.

Robinson tossed the ball hard at Woolridge and moved toward him. The other players kept the two of them apart.

"Watch your mouth, man," Robinson told Alvin.

Woolridge just smiled back at him.

"Play it cool," LaMont told Alvin.

"Next time force the ball hog down to the basket," Brian told Woolridge as the Patriots set up their offense. "I'll give him a basketball sand-wich."

On offense again, Terry and Alvin passed the ball around the Bearcats' zone defense while Brian, LaMont, and Clarence tried to get open under the hoop. As Brian faked and feinted, Gaines and the other Boorman defenders elbowed him.

Finally Brian faked a cut to the outside and then stepped back toward the basket, leaving the Boorman center behind. Terry lobbed an alley-oop pass above the rim to Brian. He caught it with both hands and slammed through the hoop.

The cheers of the Patriots' fans shook the rafters of the Butler fieldhouse.

"In your face," Brian told Gaines as he ran past.

On defense, Brian began playing away from Gaines, who wasn't much of a scoring threat. As Robinson flashed a few more shake-and-bake dribbling moves and raced past both Alvin and Terry, Brian stepped away from Gaines and leaped toward the driving six-three guard.

Robinson drove down the lane, saw Brian, and jumped, hanging in the air for what seemed like a minute.

Brian tried to block his shot, but swatted only air.

Robinson released his shot just before his feet touched the court, and the ball spun off the backboard and fell into the basket. Brian bumped him slightly and was called for a foul.

"Nice block, big guy," Robinson said to Brian, smiling as he walked to the free-throw line. The speedy guard swished his foul shot, making the score Boorman 23 and the Patriots 22.

The two teams traded baskets for most of the second quarter. Brian was open for three easy jumpers over Gaines. LaMont drove around Lance Petty for a couple of baskets, and Terry made a long three-pointer against Robinson. George Ross replaced Reed and made three jumpers in a row.

For Boorman, Robinson continued his one-man assault on the Patriots. He drove for two more hoops against Alvin, who quickly joined Reggie on the bench after fouling for the third time. Lance Petty, the Bearcats' six-four forward, swished three jump shots over Ross and LaMont. Even Gaines scored as he tapped in one of Robinson's missed shots.

At half time, Jefferson led by one, 43–42.

"We're in a dogfight now," Coach Ford said as the Patriots toweled off in the dungeonlike locker room.

"Somebody better stop Robinson," Coach Williams said, checking the scorebook. "Dude scored twenty-seven points."

"Double-team him when you can," Coach Ford said, "or force him under the hoop and let Davis have him."

"Come on, guys," LaMont shouted at the Patriots, "we already beat better teams than these dudes."

Brian and his teammates returned for the third quarter with fire in their eyes. It showed right away in their hustle.

After a Boorman player tossed the ball in to Robinson, Reggie hounded him into throwing a wild pass that Clarence intercepted. The Patriots ran a perfect three-man fast break, and Brian laid in the ball over Gaines.

Reggie guarded Robinson so closely on the following inbounds play that the Bearcats couldn't get him the ball. They tried a pass to Lance Petty, but LaMont sliced between the six-four forward and the basket and stole the ball.

"LaMont!" shouted Brian, cutting to the hoop.

Robinson tried to guard Brian, but LaMont launched a soft lob pass out of his reach. Brian caught the ball, dribbled to the basket, and jumped to slam in a two-handed tomahawk dunk so hard the backboard shook.

The action was fast after that. In the final four minutes left to play in the third quarter, the Patriots led 64–44. Boorman called time out.

The Jefferson fans gave Brian and the Patriots a standing ovation as they trotted over to their bench.

Jefferson's rally broke Boorman's spirit. Reggie and Alvin held Robinson to only thirteen points in the last quarter, and the rest of the Patriots overmatched the other Bearcats.

With only twenty-five seconds remaining in the fourth quarter and the Patriots leading by eighteen points, Brian watched Robinson fake Alvin out of his socks. He drove unguarded down the middle of the foul lane.

At the last moment, Brian switched away from Gaines and waited to block Robinson's shot. The Bearcats' tricky guard drove toward the basket, faked several times with the ball, and hung in the air.

Brian waited until just before Robinson touched the court, forced to shoot. Then he reached up and slapped the ball away from the basket and over to Terry, who dribbled until the final buzzer sounded.

"Great block!" Reggie shouted, hugging Brian.

The Jefferson fans ran onto the court and patted the Patriots on the back. Jefferson won 98–80 and eliminated Boorman from the tournament. The Patriots advanced to their next game against the Baptist Broncos on Friday.

Back in the locker room, Brian bashed forearms with his teammates.

"Man, Robinson got forty points but Davis scored forty-three," Reggie said, checking the scorebook.

"Way to play, homeboy," Clarence said, pulling off his goggles. "You don't need a backup."

Brian just nodded and slumped onto a bench. He had played the entire game and was exhausted.

FIVE

"Nice game, Davis."

"You guys looked awesome."

It was the day after the Boorman game, and Brian and the other Patriots were being welcomed at school like conquering heroes.

"Nothing beats winning," Tony said as he walked with Brian and Reggie in the hallway.

"We haven't won anything yet," Brian said. "We still gotta beat two more teams."

"Yeah, but it's great to be a hero," Tony said with a smile on his face.

"Man, we should've won a lot easier than we did last night," Reggie said. "We made Boorman look good."

"Don't blame me," Brian said, nudging Reggie playfully. "I wasn't guarding Robinson."

"Thanks a lot, man," Reggie said as they entered English class.

At practice, Coach Ford wasn't pleased, either.

"We won the game," he told the Patriots, "but our defense was terrible."

"Robinson's a super player," Coach Williams added in his baritone voice, "but we gave the other dudes too many easy shots."

"If we do that against a good team," Coach Ford said, "they'll blow us out."

"So," Coach Williams said, smiling at the players, "it's drill time again."

Some of the Patriots groaned.

"Coach's right," LaMont said. "Our defense stinks and the only way to fix it is to run some drills."

"Not only that," Coach Ford added, "but we gotta play *smarter* defense. don't let guys drive around you."

"And move your feet," Coach Williams said, "like you dudes are gonna do right now.

The players booed, then spent an hour running zigzag defensive-stance drills and footwork drills.

"Man, this is tougher than the games," Clarence said.

"That's the idea, Reed," Coach Williams said. "Compared to our practices, the games are a snap."

"You got that right," Reggie said, wiping sweat from his face with his practice jersey.

Halfway through the workout, Coach Ford stepped over to Brian, who was struggling through the drills.

"Take a break, Davis," the coach said. "You played longer than anybody last night."

"Thanks, I need it," Brian said, huffing and puffing as he sat back on the bleachers.

"But don't get too comfortable," Coach Ford

added with a smile. "You gotta work a little with Logan after practice. You know, show him some of your tricks."

"I knew there was a catch," Brian said with a smile. "You give me a break, then work me extra."

"Don't complain—you're a star," Tony shouted as he dribbled past them.

Brian shook his head and Coach Ford laughed. Practice finished with some free-throw shooting, and Coach Ford's favorite reminder for the Patriots.

"Defense wins championships," the coach said, "so be ready to bust your butts on these drills again tomorrow."

"Thanks, Coach, we're looking forward to it," Terry said a he finished his foul shots.

After most of the players left the court, Brian and Eddie Logan worked with Coach Williams for a while.

"Watch how Davis moves on offense. Practice the leg hook and jab step. Learn how to get the opposing center off balance."

Brian played one on one against the skinny freshman center, and after a while he saw some progress in Eddie Logan's offensive moves to the hoop.

"Keep working," Brian said, "and you'll make it."

"Thanks," Eddie said in a soft voice. "I got a long way to go."

"Yeah, but we might need you sooner than you think," Coach Williams said as they walked to the locker room.

Brian saw a look of terror pass over Eddie's face.

Thursday's practice began with a visit from a local TV sports crew. They wanted something strange: a different look at the Patriots.

"The whole city knows about Brian Davis," the TV announcer told the Patriots, "and he's a super player. But now we want to talk with the guys who don't get all the attention."

"Naw, you don't want to meet 'em," Brian said, laughing at his teammates. "Take my word on it."

"To know us is to love us," Terry said.

"Man, what's to love," Clarence said, shoving Terry playfully.

Everybody laughed, then the interviews began.

Brian had been interviewed a lot since his arrival in the city last summer, and his teammates had always tried to make him laugh. Now it was Brian's turn, and he loved it.

"Man, you made me crack up," Reggie told Brian.

"My mom's gonna kill me when she sees that, thanks to you, Davis," Terry said, punching Brian's arm in jest. When the TV crew left, Coach Ford called B-team coach, Pat Young, into the gym. The redheaded history teacher was the varsity's scout.

"Coach Young'll watch all our future opponents," the head coach said, "and give us a report on each of 'em."

"Man, there can't be much to say about Baptist," Reggie said, laughing. "Those dudes stink."

"How did they beat Northport?" Terry asked.

"Must've been a miracle," Tony added.

"They did it with lots of hustle," Coach Young said, adjusting his thick-rimmed glasses and looking down at his clipboard. "Northport was over-confident and got beat."

"Never get too cocky or you'll lose," Coach Williams said. "In a tourney, almost anything can happen."

Brian saw some serious looks return to his teammates' faces. They turned their attention to Coach Young.

"Baptist looks bad on paper," the redheaded B-team coach said, "but games aren't won or lost on paper."

"This is tournament time," Coach Ford added, "and everybody hustles. Even little schools like Baptist."

"But, man, we're awesome," Cisco said, smiling.

"We can be," Coach Ford said quickly, "if we hustle and think. Now listen to this scouting report."

"Baptist has one good player," Coach Young began, "and all the others are just average."

"Sorta like us," Terry said, smiling. "It's me and these other guys."

The Patriots shoved Hanson mirthfully, and Coach Ford shook his head.

"The guy's name is Nathan Steele, and he's a six-two white playmaker with good moves," said the redheaded coach. "But Dupree oughta handle him."

"Man, anything'll be easier than running after Robinson the other night," Reggie said, shaking his head.

"I hear you, bro," Alvin said, bashing forearms with Reggie. "You and me looked at the dude's heels all game."

"Steele's not as good as Robinson," Coach

Young added, "but the kid likes to shoot from the top of the key if you let him."

"He's yours, Dupree," Coach Ford said. "Stop him."

"No sweat," Reggie said, nodding.

"Baptist has only two other guys worth mentioning," Coach Young said, adjusting his thick-rimmed glasses. "Six-four black forward Manny Knox and six-five white center Jeremy Thatcher. Neither of 'em do much on offense."

"Brian oughta have fun with Thatcher," LaMont said. "The dude's a slow, fat guy who can't jump."

"Knox ain't much better," Clarence added. "I know the dude from the neighborhood. He don't like to mix it up under the boards, so put a body on him and rebound."

"Finally," Coach Young said, putting away his clipboard, "Baptist is a very slow team. We can press 'em all over the court. They're bad ball handlers, too."

"Thanks, Coach," Coach Ford said, "I'm sure the guys are looking forward to working hard today on the press."

"It's drill time," Coach Williams added with a smile.

The Patriots groaned, then started their laps around the floor.

Following a tough practice during which they worked on their full-court presses, the Patriots finished with the usual huddle and a loud team shout.

"Remember, we play the six-thirty game tomorrow night," Coach Ford yelled as Brian and his teammates left the court. "Be here at five for the bus trip to the fieldhouse."

After showering and dressing, Brian, Tony, and Reggie were walking home when suddenly Tony looked at his watch.

"Hey, it's almost time for the six-o'clock sports on TV," he said. "Our interviews!"

"Man, it's my television debut," Reggie said, laughing.

"We'll never make it home in time," Brian said.

"Mr. Riley always watches the news," Tony said, walking faster toward the nearby Seven-Eleven store.

"The dude'll change his mind about givin' us free munchies after he sees us on the tube," Reggie said. "We look like geeks."

"Speak for yourself, Dupree," Tony said.

Brian laughed and followed his friends into the local Seven-Eleven. Mr. Riley was watching the news on a TV over the counter, and he looked up when the Patriots arrived.

"The man says your interviews are coming up next," Mr. Riley said, smiling at Brian and his friends. The balding store manager reached up and increased the TV's volume.

"Hey, we won the other night," Tony said, ripping open a Milky Way. "You gonna buy us this candy?"

"You boys gotta win the sectional first," Mr. Riley said with a smile. "That was the deal."

"No sweat," Reggie said, popping the top of a Coke can. "We gonna come here and party."

The sports announcer appeared on the TV screen.

"*Shh*, here come the interviews," Tony said, pointing at the TV. "We're gonna be famous."

The announcer talked briefly about the other tournament games, then said he had some interviews with the Jefferson Patriots, one of Indianapolis's best boys' teams.

"As most of you know, Jefferson's Brian Davis is one of the best players in Indiana," the announcer said.

"Davis, my main man," Reggie said, bashing forearms with Brian.

"*Shh,*" Tony said, "I might be next."

"But basketball is a team sport, and the Jefferson High Patriots have more than just one good player. We talked today with some of the Patriots' other players, ones who don't usually get much attention from the media."

Reggie's face appeared on the screen.

"Hey, Dupree, it's you!" Mr. Riley said, smiling.

Reggie answered some of the TV announcer's brief questions in a low, mumbling voice.

"Man, I sound terrible," Reggie said, shaking his head. "That's embarrassing."

Interviews with LaMont, Clarence, and Terry followed. Then the announcer switched to other sports news.

"What?" Tony said, gesturing at the TV. "What about my interview? The dude talked to me for five minutes."

"He only showed the important guys," Reggie said, laughing and shoving Tony playfully.

"They didn't have time for everybody, Zarella," Brian said. "Maybe they'll show yours at eleven o'clock."

Tony shook his head and looked disappointed.

"Here," Mr. Riley said, slapping a Milky Way on

the counter, "this one's on me, Tony. To me, you're a star."

"Cheer up, Zarella," Reggie said as they left the Seven-Eleven, "it's not every day Mr. Riley hands out candy."

"Thanks, Mr. Riley," Tony said, ripping open the Milky Way. "Folks in Indianapolis missed a super interview."

Brian and Reggie shoved Tony, and they all laughed.

The three friends headed for home in different directions. As Brian approached his aunt's house, he saw Mo Gernert get out of a new, white Cadillac. The sharply dressed man adjusted his wire-rimmed glasses and walked over to Brian.

"Great game against Boorman, Brian," Gernert said, extending his hand. "You boys are gonna go far this year."

"Thanks," Brian said, shaking hands.

He felt something in Gernert's palm, and when Brian finished shaking he looked at his own hand and saw Gernert had give him a brand-new hundred-dollar bill.

Not understanding, Brian looked up at Gernert.

"For doing such a great job," the slick dresser said, an oily smile on his face. "There's lots more where that came from."

"But . . .?" Brian asked.

"Don't worry," Gernert said, "it's legal." He patted Brian on the arm. "I'm just a patriots fan who wants to show his appreciation. Spend it any way you want."

"I don't know," Brian started to say.

"Enjoy it, son. I'll see you around," Gernert said as he walked to his parked Cadillac. "I can help you, Brian. I got lotsa connections in big-time college ball."

Gernert got into his car and drove away, leaving Brian confused and holding one hundred dollars.

SIX

"What should I do?" Brian asked his mom and aunt at breakfast on Friday. "A hundred bucks is a lot."

"Keep the money," Aunt Margaret said as she handed a plate of pancakes to Brian. "We sure can use it."

"Yeah, but I feel funny about this Gernert guy," Brian said, sipping some orange juice. "Who is he? And why would he give me money?"

"Did he ask you to do anything for him?" Brian's mom asked. She sat across from Brian and was dressed for her job as a bookkeeper at a downtown medical clinic.

"Naw, he just said it was for doing a great job in the Boorman game."

"Lotsa money changes hands during tournament time," Aunt Margaret said, sipping her coffee. "Heck, every office in Indianapolis has a pool on the game."

"Yeah, but what if this Gernert fella is bad?" Brian asked, forking some pancakes into his mouth.

"You said he looked okay," Brian's mom said, getting ready to leave with his aunt, who also worked at the medical clinic. "Maybe you're just overreacting, Brian."

"Maybe he really does want to help you," his aunt said. "Besides, there ain't no law against giving kids money."

"Why don't you ask Coach Ford about it?" his mom said, setting her coffee cup in the sink.

"Naw, maybe you're right," Brian said, wiping his lips with a paper napkin. "It's probably nothing."

Still, Brian hid the hundred-dollar bill in his desk drawer at home. He decided not to tell anybody about it, even Tony and Reggie.

That night, twelve thousand fans packed Butler University's fieldhouse for the sectional semifinal games.

"Man, we draw crowds," Reggie said. He and the Patriots were changing into their blue uniforms in the dungeonlike locker room. "They wanna see us destroy Baptist."

"We can do it," Coach Williams said. "These Baptist guys are inexperienced."

"If we press 'em," Coach Ford said in his final instructions, "they'll panic and throw bad passes."

LaMont led the Patriots onto the fieldhouse court and their four thousand fans stood and cheered. Jefferson's pep band was the one chosen for this night's games, and while the two teams warmed up they played some spirited instrumentals.

The buzzer sounded, and the starting lineups were introduced to the fans. Then Brian and the four usual starters huddled around the coaches near their bench.

"Press these guys," Coach Ford said, "and remember, we play one game at a time. Don't look forward to tomorrow's finals."

"Ready," LaMont said, "one, two, three, let's go!"

The team raised hands and broke the huddle. Brian and the starting five then walked to the midcourt jump-ball circle and shook hands with the Baptist starters, who wore white uniforms trimmed with red and gold.

One of the refs tossed up the ball between Brian and Baptist's fat center, Jeremy Thatcher. Brian easily out-jumped Thatcher and tapped the ball to Terry, who dribbled toward the Patriots' basket.

"They're playing man to man," LaMont shouted to the others. "Set up the offense."

Brian ran under the hoop and waited for Clarence to set a pick behind Thatcher, who seemed a little lost. Brian faked toward the hoop, then cut around Reed's solid pick to the free-throw line. Terry zipped a pass to him.

Davis caught the ball, turned, and swished a fifteen-foot jump shot. Jefferson's cheerleaders jumped along the sidelines, and their rooters cheered in the stands.

"Way to shoot, homeboy," Clarence said, bashing forearms with Brian.

"Pick 'em up!" LaMont shouted, running into a full-court-press position. "Get in their jocks!"

"I got Steele," Reggie said, crouching and playing up on Baptist's best player.

Brian watched from midcourt as the Patriots pressed the Broncos all over the floor. Steele tried dribbling against Reggie, but couldn't get past the ten-second line.

"Hey!" shouted Thatcher, waving his hands.

Steele lofted a long pass toward Thatcher just across the midcourt line. Brian waited until the ball was in the air, then leaped in front of the overweight Baptist Center and stole the pass.

"Davis!" shouted Reggie, cutting to the hoop.

Brian fired a chest pass to Dupree, who missed a lay-up. Manny Knox, Baptist's six-four black forward, tried to rebound, but Clarence blocked him away from the basket.

Reed grabbed the ball and laid it in, smacking Knox on the head with his elbow at the same time. It wasn't a foul, but the Broncos' forward made a face and rubbed his head.

"Nice boards, Reed," Brian said, bashing forearms.

"That dude hates contact," Clarence said, smiling at Brian. "He won't rebound much from now on."

The Patriots continued to steal the ball and turn the Broncos' mistakes into hoops. When the Baptist coach finally called a time-out after four minutes, Jefferson led 16–2. The Broncos' only points came on a jumper by Steele.

"Keep the pressure on 'em," LaMont told the Patriots as they walked back onto the floor after the time-out.

"Let's double-team 'em in the backcourt," Reggie told the others. "Make 'em cough up the ball."

The double team worked, and Terry stole the ball from Steele near the ten-second line.

"Set up the offense," Terry shouted, passing to Reggie as they waited for Brian to run into position.

Terry shouted out a play number, and the Patriots set a pick for Brian. Thatcher, red in the face and breathing hard, cut Brian off as he tried to run across the lane. Brian faked in that direction, then cut back door to the basket.

Reggie lobbed an alley-oop pass above the hoop. Brian caught the pass with both hands and slammed it through the basket just as Manny Knox tried to block the shot. The six-four Baptist forward ducked, but still got smacked in the face with the ball as it swished through the hoop.

The Patriots' fans went wild. As Brian ran downcourt he raised his fist in triumph.

Jefferson led after the first quarter 23–10. Only three jump shots by Steele kept Baptist in the game.

"Great defense, guys," Coach Ford said.

"Man, let's keep it up," Reggie said, toweling off.

Both teams kept the same lineups to start the second quarter. Baptist didn't have many good subs.

"We can wear these guys down," Brian told Hanson as they walked onto the court.

"Yeah, Thatcher's about had it now," Terry said, looking at the Broncos' fat center. "Let's run some breaks."

Many Knox inbounded the ball to Nathan Steele, and Reggie hounded him immediately.

"Come on, hotshot," Reggie said, slapping at the ball as Steele dribbled, "show me something."

Despite Reggie's pressure defense, the Broncos managed to set up their half-court offense. Brian guarded Thatcher so closely that the blubbery center eventually stopped running and just leaned on him.

"Hey, ref, look at this," Brian said, shoving against the two-hundred-fifty-pound Thatcher's back.

"What's the matter, Davis, can't you take a hint?"

Brian turned and saw Manny Knox. He was using Thatcher's body to pick off LaMont and receive a pass from Steele.

"Switch!" LaMont yelled. He took the exhausted Thatcher, and Brian jumped out to guard Knox.

"Come on, stop me if you can," Knox said. The black forward faked with the ball, then drove to the hoop.

Brian let Knox cut a step ahead of him, then waited for his lay-up shot. He blocked the ball off Knox's face and over to Terry.

The Patriots' fans cheered the play, and Brian saw the shocked expression on Knox's face.

"Eat that," Brian told Knox as they ran downcourt.

On offense, Reggie dribbled toward the basket and let Steele smash into the pick Brian was making. Brian watched as Reggie stepped behind the three-point circle and swished a long jumper. Jefferson now led 26–10.

The Patriots continued to press the Broncos all over the court, but Steele got the ball into the half-court area. Brian tried to guard Thatcher, but the big center was leaning all his weight back onto him again.

"Foul," Brian shouted, "he's fouling me."

It was hard work holding up the fat center, and since the refs weren't calling a foul, Brian thought of a way to get back at Thatcher. He let him catch a pass, and when Thatcher leaned backward with all his weight, Brian stepped quickly aside. Thatcher lost his balance and fell back onto his butt.

The refs whistled him for traveling, and the Jefferson rooters cheered.

"I'll get you for that," Thatcher told Brian as he stood, his fat face red with anger.

"Stop leaning on me and I won't do it again," Brian replied. "You've been fouling me all game."

Thatcher still held on to the ball, and now he tossed it at Brian and hit him in the head.

"Hey!" Clarence shouted.

The players on the court gathered around, and before any further trouble started one of the refs stepped in and looked at Thatcher.

"Son, you're outta the game," said the ref, pointing to the sidelines. "That's unsportsmanlike behavior."

The Jefferson fans stomped on the bleachers, and the Baptist rooters booed the refs. Thatcher just glared at Brian and walked over to the Broncos' bench, where he kicked a towel.

A six-three reserve center entered the game for Baptist, and the play continued.

On defense for the Patriots, Brian blocked a driving lay-up shot by Steele and a short jumper by Knox. Clarence blocked three more of the Broncos' shots during the rest of the quarter.

"Man, you guys are the Jefferson 'swat' team,"

Reggie said after Brian blocked another of Steele's shots.

On offense, the Patriots scored often on fast-break lay-ups after steals and blocked shots. At half time, they led 43–24. Playing the entire game so far, Brian scored sixteen points and LaMont added fourteen.

"We gotta work harder on defense in the second half," Coach Ford told the Patriots in their locker room.

"Shut these guys down," Coach Williams added, "don't let 'em score a basket without working for it."

"We're leading by almost twenty points, Coach," Reggie said, "ain't that enough?"

"Sure it is," Coach Ford said, "but let's use an easy game like this to get ready for the tougher teams."

"Play the defense we worked on this week," Coach Williams added.

"Sounds cool," Reed said, pulling off his protective goggles. "Besides, I like blocking the shots."

The Patriots opened the third quarter by showing the twelve thousand fans in Butler's fieldhouse what tough defense was.

"Pick up your men," LaMont shouted to the Patriots as they watched Baptist inbound the ball, "and stay with 'em."

Before Nathan Steele could dribble to the ten-second line, Reggie and Terry double-teamed him and stole the ball. Terry dribbled in for an unguarded lay-up.

The Broncos tried to work the ball downcourt again, but Clarence leaped and intercepted a pass near the sideline. He passed the ball to Reggie, who floated a return pass above the Patriot's rim. Reed soared off the court, caught the pass, and slammed the ball down through the basket.

The Patriots' rooters stood and cheered, and Brian bashed forearms with Clarence.

"Way to sky, bro," Brian said.

The third quarter was a rout for the Patriots. Brian blocked a shot by Knox and stole the ball from the center. All of Jefferson's players worked hard on defense, including George, Alvin, and the other subs who played the last few minutes of the third quarter.

The Patriots held Baptist to only eight points in the quarter, and after three periods led 75–32.

"That was our best defense of the season," Coach Ford told the team between quarters.

"Yeah, we smoked 'em," Terry said, bashing forearms with his teammates. "We're in the finals tomorrow!"

"Man, we're headin' for the Final Four!" Reggie said.

Coach Ford cleared the bench for the fourth quarter, giving Brian and the other starters a rest. Even Eddie Logan saw his first action and played center for the rest of the game.

The Patriot starters enjoyed Eddie's first game.

"Almost, Eddie," Brian shouted with a smile as Logan tried for a rebound but lost it to George Ross.

"Don't let him push you around, Logan," La-Mont shouted when the skinny freshman center caught Manny Knox's elbow in his chest. "Give it back to him."

And Brian felt like a proud teacher when Eddie

hauled in a rebound and started a Patriots' fast break.

The game ended with the score Jefferson 87 and Baptist 50. Brian led the Patriots with twenty-two points. He blocked four shots. Clarence blocked seven shots.

The Baptist Broncos, their season over, shook hands with Brian and the Patriots.

"Let's stay and watch the next game to see who we're gonna play tomorrow," Brian said as the Patriots dressed in the locker room. "I think it'll be Eastside."

But the Quiller Chargers used accurate outside shooting and some hustling defense to upset Eastside, 75–72.

"Man, those Quiller dudes play dirty," Reggie said as they filed out of Butler's fieldhouse with the crowd.

"So do their fans," Tony said. "They were throwing stuff at the Eastside bench all night."

"Good," Brian said, feeling as tired as he had all season. "Less to throw at us when we beat them tomorrow night."

SEVEN

"Man, I hate morning practices," Reggie said, walking onto the Jefferson High court.

"Especially Saturday-morning practices," Tony added.

"What's the matter, Zarella, missing your cartoons?" Terry said, warming up with his ball at a main basket.

"He's missing his sleep," Brian said, lazily shooting a short jumper at the hoop. "Me, too." He yawned.

Coach Ford called the rare morning practice to go over the scouting report for the Quiller Chargers, their opponent at eight o'clock that evening.

"You look tired, Davis," Coach Williams said as he entered the gym with Coach Ford.

"You'd be tired, too, if that lump Thatcher leaned on you for half the game," Brian said, smiling.

The players and coaches laughed, then met at

the midcourt jump-ball circle. B-team coach Pat Young, carrying a clipboard, joined them from the downstairs locker room.

"Every tourney game is important," Coach Ford said, "but tonight's game is something special."

"After tonight, only sixty-four teams will be left in the state tournament," Coach Williams added. "Then the real fun starts, and the teams get tougher."

"But first, we gotta beat Quiller," Coach Ford said.

"And don't think their win over Eastside was a big upset," Coach Williams said. "The dudes can play ball."

"So can we," Terry said, nodding his head.

"Yeah, we're the best team in the city," Tony added.

"In the state," Brian said, smiling at his teammates.

LaMont started clapping, slowly at first, then faster as all the Patriots joined in, their applause echoing in the empty gym.

"Yeah, all right!" they shouted, stopping their applause. "Jefferson, number one!"

"And I was wondering how to get you guys psyched for tonight's game," Coach Ford said.

"Man, we're always psyched," Reggie said.

"Good, let's be prepared, too," Coach Ford said, nodding at B-team coach Young.

"Quiller's a tough team with five good starters," the redheaded coach said, pushing his glasses onto the bridge of his nose. "They out-rebounded almost every team they played this year."

"Those dudes ain't very big," Clarence said.

"No, but they're mean," Coach Williams said.

"Right," continued Coach Young." They hit the boards hard on both defense and offense, and their man-to-man defense is one of the best I've seen."

"It's dirty," Terry said. "They slap and push a lot."

"Yeah, and they like to swing their elbows, too," Tony added. "Last night, they nearly took a kid's head off."

"I'll get on the refs about it," Coach Ford promised, "but you guys just play ball and forget it."

"Yeah, some teams try to pick fights with the other team's best player," Coach Williams said. "Then the refs toss both 'em outta the game.

"Quiller's best player is their six-six center, Rodney Garrett," Coach Young continued. He looked up at Brian. "He's a black kid who likes to mix it up."

"Dude's real active on offense, too," Coach Williams added. "Don't go for his fakes, Davis."

"And block him away from the boards," Coach Ford said. "If Quiller out-rebounds us, it'll be tough to beat 'em."

"Coach, you make these guys sound like champs," Terry said. "They're just punks from the Northside."

"They're not champs," Coach Young said, adjusting his thick-rimmed glasses, "but their starters play hard all four quarters. That's their weak spot. They don't have any good subs."

"Quiller's lost nine games this season," Coach Ford said, "and every loss came after their starters got tired or fouled out. If we wear 'em down, they're hurting."

"Clancy Drew, a five-nine black playmaker, runs their offense," Coach Young said, checking his clipboard. "He's a fancy passer, so be ready on defense. He whips behind-the-back and between-the-leg passes all the time."

"Dude's good," Reggie said, nodding. "Got fast hands on defense, too. He's so little, he sneaks up on you."

"Take him, Reg," Coach Ford said.

"You other guys watch out," Coach Williams added. "If Drew has the ball, be ready for a quick pass to your man."

"Quiller's other starters aren't bad, either," Coach Young continued. "Allan Dishman, a six-five white forward, is an animal on the boards. You gotta block him out."

"Reed can handle him," Alvin said. "He's an animal, too." Woolridge bashed forearms with Clarence.

"I hope so," Coach Young added, "because their other forward, a six-three white kid named Tracy Madison, crashes the boards, too. Their other guard, a six-two white kid named Tommy Sanders, grabs his share of rebounds."

"This ain't gonna be a picnic, guys," Coach Williams said. "It's the sectional finals, and any team that makes it this far's gotta be pretty good, even if they're punks."

Brian saw the nervous looks on his teammates' faces and felt his own nerves churning in his stomach.

The Patriots spent an hour working against Quiller's favorite offenses and defenses, then quit at one o'clock.

"Get some rest this afternoon," Coach Ford told them as they left the gym. "Be back here at six."

"Quiller sounds pretty good," Tony said as he walked from the gym with Reggie and Brian.

"We can handle 'em," Brian said, hoping his voice didn't reveal how nervous he really was.

"Yeah, I'm psyched," Reggie said. "I just hate waitin' around home until game time."

"How about lunch at the mall?" Tony asked.

"Okay, I want to buy some tunes at Music-World," Reggie said, checking the money in his wallet.

"Look who's loaded," Brian said, smiling as he peeked at Dupree's billfold. "Dude's buying lunch today."

Brian and Tony shoved Reggie, and they all laughed.

After burgers and fries at the Hamburger Heaven in the new Eastgate Mall, Brian and his two friends spent an hour at MusicWorld, where Reggie bought a discounted rap tape.

"Hey, look," Tony said, pointing at a Maple Farms ice-cream shop as they headed home. "Ain't that where Vanos is working now? I heard he got a job cleaning tables."

"That's the place," Reggie said, looking inside the crowded shop. "And there's Nick."

Brian looked toward the back of the ice-cream shop and saw Nick Vanos clearing some dirty dishes from a table.

"Hey, man," Reggie said as the three Patriots stepped over to Nick, "like your uniform."

Nick looked up and seemed surprised, and a bit

embarrassed, to see his former teammates. He wiped his hands on his stained apron and started to high-five Reggie.

"Man, you only been away from the team a few days and already you forgot we don't do that no more," Reggie said, bashing forearms with Nick. "That's my man."

"What's happening?" Nick said, bashing forearms with Brian and Tony, too. "You guys oughta be home resting up for the big game tonight. I hear Quiller ain't bad."

"Ice cream's our new training food," Tony said with a big smile on his stubbled face.

"Yeah, especially now that we got us a connection at this Maple Farms shop," Brian said. "How's the job?"

"Not bad," Nick said, shrugging his shoulders. "Coach Ford helped me get it a few days ago. But I miss playing."

Brian, Reggie, and Tony sat at the table Nick had been clearing off, and ordered three ice-cream sundaes. After the ice cream arrived, Brian heard a voice calling his name.

"Davis stinks," called a voice from a corner table.

"Yeah, and Jefferson ain't got a chance tonight," another voice said. "We're gonna kick their butts."

"That's because they're a bunch of wimps," shouted a third voice, laughing with his buddies.

"What the . . .?" Reggie asked, looking up from his butterscotch sundae.

Brian and his two teammates turned and saw three guys and two girls laughing at them. The boys wore Quiller jackets and the girls were carrying blue-and-gold pom-poms.

"Man, even Quiller's fans are punks," Reggie said.

"Just ignore 'em," Brian said, turning his attention to the hot fudge sundae in front of him.

"We gotta beat Quiller and show those jerks they're not as cool as they think," Tony said.

The three Patriots ate their ice cream and talked among themselves until a rolled-up napkin thrown by the Quiller kids landed in Brian's sundae. The five kids burst into laughter.

"Damn," Reggie said, starting to get up.

"I'll handle it," Nick said, walking over from where he'd been cleaning another table.

"Watch that hot temper of yours," Brian told Nick.

"Yeah, you don't wanna lose your job," Tony said.

"I've learned my lesson," Nick said, walking over to the shop's manager.

Brian watched as the stern-faced manager kicked the Quiller kids out of the store.

"No more fights for me," Nick said as he returned to his old teammates. He looked away. "Booze used to get me so ticked off I wanted to beat the crap outta everybody."

A strained silence surrounded the four Jefferson kids.

"Yeah, but you trashed these Quiller kids for us," Reggie said, bashing forearms with Nick as Brian and his teammates got ready to head for home. "Thanks, man."

"Once a Patriot, always a Patriot," Brian said.

"Thanks," Nick said. "Good luck tonight."

"We'll kick a few butts for you, Vanos," Tony said.

They all laughed, and the three Patriots left.

"I can hardly wait until tonight," Tony said as they walked through their neighborhood.

"Yeah, I really dig playing in championship games," Reggie added. "Last one for me was back in middle school."

"We won our sectional at Paintville last year," Brian said, remembering the thrill.

"That don't count," Reggie said. "It was down on the farm." He playfully nudged Brian and laughed.

"Hey, I been thinking about this," Tony said. "Every hoop's a big one during a championship game."

"Every rebound, too," Brian added. "That's why they call 'em pressure games."

"Stop it, guys," Reggie said, "I'm getting psyched and it's only three o'clock."

Brian and Tony laughed and shoved Reggie.

They were almost at Aunt Margaret's two-story house when Brian turned and saw Mo Gernert drive up and stop his new white Cadillac beside them.

"Hi, boys." He adjusted his wire-rimmed glasses and looked up at them. "Want a ride home? You shouldn't be walking on game day."

Brian saw Reggie and Tony look up at him, puzzled expressions on their faces.

"No, thanks," Brian told Gernert in a thin, nervous voice. "We got only a few more blocks to go."

"Suit yourselves," Gernert said, smiling. "Good luck tonight. Could be the most important game of your life, Davis." He closed his window and drove down the street.

Brian felt uncomfortable.

"Who was that?" Tony asked, watching the white Cadillac turn a corner. "Reminds me of a gangster on TV."

"Who cares?" Reggie said. "The dude drives a mean machine."

Brian stopped walking and took a deep breath. He had to tell somebody about Wright and Gernert. The pressure was too much, especially with the team playing big games.

He looked at Reggie and Tony and told them everything.

"Man, what do you think the dude wants?" Reggie asked.

"I don't know," Brian said. "Maybe he's okay and just wants to find me a good college to play ball."

"You gonna keep the hundred bucks?" Tony asked.

"I'll take it," Reggie said, laughing.

"Get serious, Dupree," Tony said.

"Why?" Reggie said, shrugging. "This Gernert dude ain't busted no laws. I think Brian's worrying for nothin'."

"Maybe Reg's right," Brian said. "Guess I'll keep the money and spend it when I think it's okay."

"Yeah, like on our victory party after tonight. Right, Zarella?"

"I can taste the pizza now. . . ."

"Dream on," Brian said, trying not to look worried.

EIGHT

"At least we got a better locker room tonight," Terry said as the Patriots dressed in their white uniforms for the championship game.

"Yeah, but it's still cold in here," Clarence said, adjusting his goggles. "The whole fieldhouse is cold."

Brian pulled on his jersey and saw the determined looks on the Patriots' faces.

Even the coaches looked psyched.

"All right," Coach Ford said finally, "we've talked enough. Now we're ready to play."

"Yeah, let's go, Patriots!" Cisco shouted.

The players huddled around the coaches and stuck their hands into the middle.

"Play hard and have fun," Coach Ford said as Brian and his teammates leaned so close their heads almost touched.

"Man, winnin' is the most fun," Reggie said.

"All right!" shouted several players.

"Ready," LaMont said. "One, two, three . . ."

". . . *let's go!*" shouted the players, breaking the huddle by raising their hands.

Brian and the Patriots followed LaMont up the ramp and onto the Butler fieldhouse court for their warm-ups. The old hangarlike arena was packed to the rafters with almost fifteen thousand fans. The Jefferson High rooters and the Patriots' cheerleaders, waving red-white-and-blue pom-poms, cheered along the sidelines.

The Quiller Chargers, led by their six-six center Rodney Garrett and dressed in gold warm-up suits, raced onto the court. Their several thousand fans went wild, and the Northport band, chosen for the finals, played loudly.

"The Quiller players do look like punks," Reggie told Brian as they waited in the lay-up line.

"We'll teach 'em a lesson," Brian said. The crowd and the music was getting him super-psyched, so he ran in and slam-dunked the ball.

Just before game time, LaMont met with the refs and Quiller's co-captains, Rodney Garrett and Allan Dishman.

"Man, those dudes didn't want to shake hands," LaMont told Brian and the others when he rejoined the warm-ups.

"No class," Clarence said.

The buzzer calling the teams to their benches sounded, and Brian felt a twinge of nervousness in his stomach.

The fans stood and cheered, and the cheerleaders of both schools ran onto the court for the introduction of the starting lineups. The Patriots bashed forearms and clapped as both teams were presented to the crowd.

Then Coach Ford huddled the team together in front of their bench.

"We play 'em one at a time," said the coach, "but if we don't win tonight, that's it for the season."

"We'll beat 'em, Coach," LaMont said. "Right, guys?"

Brian and his teammates shouted and clapped.

The starters for both teams walked to the midcourt jump-ball circle, and Brian extended his hand to Rodney Garrett. But the six-six center just scowled at him.

One of the refs checked with the official timer, then tossed the ball up between Brian and Garrett.

Brian leaped and reached as high as his six-foot-eight-inch frame could go, but Garrett out-jumped him and tapped the ball to Clancy Drew, Quiller's five-nine playmaker.

The Quiller rooters cheered and waved blue-and-gold pom-poms.

"Pick up your men," LaMont shouted to the Patriots.

"I got Garrett," Brian said, pointing at the Chargers' center. "Who's got Dishman?"

"Dude's mine," Clarence said, running down-court and guarding the six-five white forward closely.

"I got the little guy," Reggie said, crouching into a defensive stance and guarding Drew, who was dribbling.

Under Quiller's basket, Brian tried to stay close to Garrett, but the husky black center elbowed him in the chest and the chin. Finally, Garrett faked, then cut to the free-throw line.

Drew head-faked Reggie out of position on the right side of the hoop, then whipped a blind pass to Garrett at the foul line. Brian tried to recover and catch up with Garrett, but Allan Dishman ran into him and shoved him away. Brian fell backward onto his butt.

Garrett jumped and swished a fifteen-foot jumper.

Quiller led 2–0, and their fans went wild.

"That's an offensive foul!" Coach Ford shouted at the refs. "The kid knocked Davis down!"

The refs shook their heads and play continued.

Clarence passed the ball in to Terry, who dribbled downcourt toward the Patriots' basket.

Brian shook off the pain of Garrett's elbows and the shove by Dishman to set up an offense. Quiller was playing a tight man-to-man defense, making it hard for Terry to pass the ball without having it intercepted.

He also saw the Chargers were grabbing the Patriots' uniforms and slapping their arms.

"Man, don't hold me!" Reggie said, pushing Drew away from him.

The refs blew their whistles and called a foul on Reggie. Coach Ford leaped off the bench, and Reggie held out his arms in an 'I can't believe it' gesture.

"You dudes ain't gonna get away with this dirty ball," Reggie said, pointing at Drew. Quiller's fans booed.

"Cool it, Dupree," LaMont said as the Patriots set up their man-to-man defense. "We'll get our breaks."

The Chargers ran downcourt and set up their offense. Drew tricky-dribbled away from Reggie, then tossed a sharp chest pass to Dishman on the right side of the basket. Rodney Garrett pushed

Brian just enough to get free, then caught Dishman's overhead pass in the lane.

"Switch!" Brian shouted, taking LaMont's man while he jumped over and guarded Garrett.

But it was too late. Garrett was already in the air, and he swished another jumper.

The score wâs now Quiller 4 and Jefferson 0.

"Fight through those picks," LaMont told Brian and the Patriots. "We can't give 'em open shots."

"The guy's pushing me every time," Brian said as he ran down to play offense.

"Push him back," Clarence said.

Brian felt his anger toward the Chargers building and he decided to get some revenge on offense.

As Reggie dribbled across midcourt, Brian ran along the base line, then cut sharply toward the free-throw line. Garrett stayed with him.

"Dupree!" Brian shouted, raising his right hand for a pass. Reggie looked the other way, then zipped a chest pass to Brian at the free-throw line.

Brian caught the ball and turned to face Garrett.

"Davis, you ain't nothing," the six-six center said.

"Lay it on him, homeboy," Clarence said.

Brian got Garrett off balance with a head fake, then dribbled between his own legs and drove for the hoop. Garrett tried to recover, but Brian leaped and slammed the ball through the basket.

"Take that, chump," Brian told Garrett.

At the Chargers' end of the floor, Dishman shot a short jumper but missed. Clarence turned to grab the rebound but forgot to block Dishman away from the hoop. Quiller's six-five power forward stepped around Reed, grabbed the loose ball, and laid it in. Clarence knocked into him for a foul.

"Man, where did the dude come from?" Reed asked as the Patriots lined up for the free throw.

"These guys are good rebounders," Brian said, "so block 'em out all the time."

Dishman swished his free throw, and the score was Quiller 7 and the Patriots 2.

Terry dribbled downcourt and called out a play. Brian faked a cut to the free-throw line and Garrett fell for it. Then Brian stepped beyond the three-point line, caught a sharp pass from Terry, and swished a long jumper.

"Way to shoot, Davis," LaMont said, bashing forearms with Brian. "Now let's pick 'em up full court."

The Patriots pressed the Chargers all over the floor. Dishman threw a wild pass to Drew and Reed stole it at midcourt. Clarence dribbled toward the hoop, but Garrett stepped in front of him and they crashed to the floor. The refs whistled a charging foul on Reed, and the Jefferson fans filled Butler's fieldhouse with a loud chorus of boos.

"Man, this is gonna be a rough game," Clarence said, readjusting his goggles after the collision.

"It's gonna be a one-sided game if the refs keep calling fouls like that," Terry said. "That wasn't a charge."

Quiller inbounded the ball again, and this time Drew dribbled it over the ten-second line and set up their offense. Brian stuck close to Garrett, who continued to elbow him in the arms and chest.

Drew held up a fist and the Chargers ran a play.

"Watch the pick, homeboy," Clarence told Brian.

Brian followed Garrett toward the free-throw line and fought through a solid pick set by Dishman. Garrett caught a pass from Drew, turned to the hoop, and shot a fifteen-foot jumper.

The ball never made it to the hoop.

Brian leaped and blocked the shot. The ball bounced to Reggie, who started a Patriots' fast break.

Coach Williams jumped for joy on the bench.

"All right, homeboy!" Reed shouted.

"In yo' face," LaMont told Garrett as the Patriots ran downcourt.

Reggie stopped at the free-throw line, looked at LaMont and Terry cutting on his left and right, then waited for the trailer. Brian ran down the lane and raised both hands.

"Dupree!" he shouted, cutting alone to the hoop.

Brian caught a scoop pass from Reggie, avoided Dishman, and laid in the ball. Dishman reached over his back and slapped him on the arm for a foul.

Brian swished his free throw, and the score was now Jefferson 8 and Quiller 7.

As they trotted downcourt, Garrett elbowed Brian.

The refs whistled Garrett for a foul.

"You think you're hot stuff, eh, Davis?" Garrett said. He stepped so close Brian could see the sweat pores on his face. "Man, I'm gonna stick you in the hoop."

"You and who else?" Brian asked, standing face-to-face with Garrett. "All you can do is foul."

The refs and both teams broke up the mini-scuffle, and the Patriots set up their offense again.

For the rest of the first quarter, the Patriots and the Chargers traded baskets. The quarter ended in a tie, 15–15. Garrett led Quiller with nine points, and Brian scored ten for Jefferson.

"Man, I'm all bruised," Reggie said as the Patriots slumped onto their bench. "Those dudes must think they're playing football."

"Yeah, look at my arms," Terry said. "I've got Dishman's fingerprints all over me."

"We're doing fine, guys," Coach Ford shouted over the loud pep-band music. "Don't let a few bumps bother you."

"Yeah, this is the sectional finals," Coach Williams reminded the players. "The tougher team is gonna win."

"And that's us," LaMont said, leading the Patriots onto the court for the second quarter.

Both starting lineups remained in the game, and Clarence passed the ball in to Terry to start the period.

Before the Patriots could set up their offense, Drew lashed out and stole the ball from Terry, then dribbled toward Quiller's basket.

Brian, still standing near midcourt, turned and raced after the five-nine playmaker. His long strides ate up the distance between them, and he caught up with Drew just as he was about to shoot a lay-up. Brian wanted to smash the ball back down the speedy guard's throat.

Davis leaped, but Drew saw him coming and spun around in a 360-degree turn, then laid in the ball. Brian sailed past him and landed harmlessly out of bounds.

The crowd erupted with a roar, and Drew ran back downcourt with his fist raised. The score was now Quiller 17, Jefferson 15.

"Let's get the points back," LaMont shouted to Brian, who felt a bit shocked by Drew's fancy move.

"Look," Reggie said as he dribbled downcourt, "they're playing a two-three zone now."

"That'll be a big mistake," Brian said, running to the base line to set up the Patriots' zone offense.

Reggie and Terry zipped the ball around the outside of Quiller's zone, until Reggie shot a jumper that missed. Brian drove around Garrett and grabbed the rebound, pump-faked once, and laid in the ball.

"All right, Davis!" Coach Williams shouted.

Quiller raced down the floor. Drew, playing with confidence after his spectacular three-sixty, tricky-dribbled past Reggie and drove down the foul lane.

Brian stayed with Garrett until the last possible moment, then leaped toward Drew and slapped his shot away.

The Jefferson rooters stood and cheered, and Drew looked around like he'd just had his pocket picked.

The Patriots started a four-on-three fast break, with Brian bringing up the rear. Reggie caught a pass from Terry about eighteen feet from the basket and launched a jumper. The ball hit the front rim and bounced high in the air. Garrett jumped too soon for the rebound.

Brian snaked through the crowd of players in the lane and tipped the missed shot into the basket.

The score was now Jefferson 19 and Quiller 17.

On defense, the Patriots fought and scrapped against Quiller's big three: Garrett, Dishman, and Drew. But with three minutes to play in the half, Brian smacked Garrett on the arm for his first foul, then did it again moments later for his second.

As Garrett shot his free throws, Brian looked at Eddie Logan on the Patriots' bench and saw the nervous look on the skinny freshman's face.

Don't worry, Eddie, Brian said to himself between free throws, *I'm through making fouls.*

But as the half wound down, and with the score 32 to 31 in favor of Quiller, Brian caught a pass from Terry and drove along the base line to the hoop.

He charged into Garrett for his third foul.

The Patriots' rooters groaned, but instead of using Eddie Logan, Coach Ford sent Alvin Woolridge into the game. Reggie moved to a forward position and Clarence played center.

"Don't let up," Brian shouted to the Patriots from the bench. "There are still twenty seconds left in the half."

Drew caught an inbounds pass from Dishman and started to set up the Chargers' offense. But with ten seconds to play, LaMont switched off Dishman and intercepted Drew's lob pass to Garrett.

"Hey!" Terry shouted, running downcourt toward the Patriots' basket.

LaMont lofted a length-of-the-court pass that Terry caught and laid in as the half-time buzzer sounded.

The basket gave the Patriots the lead, 33 to 32.

Butler's fieldhouse erupted with a loud cheer as Brian and his teammates raced off the court for the break.

The Patriots' locker room was a happy place.

"Way to play," Reggie said, bashing forearms with LaMont and Terry. "That'll show that little geek Drew."

"Let's bury 'em," Terry said.

"Game's not over yet," Coach Ford said, settling down the players. "And we're missing too many easy shots."

"We gotta stop Garrett and Dishman from getting inside position on the boards," Coach Williams added in his baritone voice. "Only Davis is working for rebounds."

"Way to hit the boards, homeboy," LaMont said.

"Yeah, now all you gotta do is hit Garrett," Reggie said. "Dude's been smacking everybody."

"I'd like to," Brian said, "but I already got three fouls."

The third quarter opened with both starting lineups on the court. Clarence passed the ball inbounds to Terry, who dribbled over the half-court line to set up the offense.

Brian ran along the base line and saw the same scowl on Rodney Garrett's face. He also felt Garrett pulling on his jersey when the refs weren't looking.

"That's a foul!" Coach Ford yelled from the bench.

Terry passed the ball to Brian in the right corner. The Patriots then cleared out and left Brian alone with Garrett, who crouched into a defensive stance. It was one on one.

Brian showed Garrett the ball, then snatched it

away when the Chargers' center swiped at it and fell off balance. Dribbling one step ahead of Garrett, who tried to grab Brian's jersey and slow him down, Davis was open for a jumper and banked a fifteen-footer off the backboard. All Garrett could do was stop and watch the ball swish through.

The quarter continued with the teams matching baskets. Drew and Dishman hit jumpers in the lane for Quiller, while Garrett continued to crash the boards. For the Patriots, Brian scored three baskets on drives past Garrett, and Reggie swished two long jumpers. Both teams scrapped on defense.

But with two minutes left in the quarter and Jefferson leading 51–47, Brian tried to block a driving lay-up shot by Dishman and fouled him on the arm. It was Brian's fourth foul, and with nearly an entire quarter remaining he was pulled from the rest of the quarter.

"Bad call," Terry said, shaking his head.

"Now what are we gonna do?" Reggie asked.

"Play tough," Brian said as he slumped onto the bench. "You guys can do it."

Coach Ford thought for a moment, then signaled for Eddie Logan to take Brian's place. The fans buzzed.

"Show 'em the moves you used against me in practice, Eddie," Brian shouted at the nervous freshman.

"Yeah, just do your best until Davis gets back," Terry said. "We'll back you up on defense."

"Is this the best you dudes can come up with?" Garrett said, laughing as he pointed at Eddie Logan.

For the last two minutes of the third quarter, Garrett and the Chargers seemed more confident with Brian on the bench. Drew passed twice to Garrett in the lane for easy baskets and Allan Dishman tapped in a missed shot. Eddie Logan seemed lost and let the Chargers push him around.

The buzzer sounded with the score tied, 53–53.

"Okay, this next quarter is for the championship," LaMont told the Patriots on the bench.

"Quiller's tired," Coach Ford said over the screams of the rival cheer blocks. "They haven't used a sub yet."

"Garrett's dragging his butt on the court he's so exhausted," Coach Williams said. "Drive on him and make the dude play defense. He'll probably foul."

"We're going with Eddie at center for a few minutes," Coach Ford said, patting Logan on the arm.

"You can do it, Eddie," Tony said, giving him the thumbs-up signal.

The other Patriots patted Logan on the back.

"Then we'll bring Brian back for crunch time," the coach said finally.

"You heard the coach," Brian told Eddie. "Drive on Garrett. Just put some moves on him."

The Patriots inbounded the ball, and immediately Terry passed to Reggie, who zipped a chest pass to Eddie on the base line. Garrett seemed to relax for a moment and Logan dribbled around him to the hoop.

Eddie made the lay-up, and Garrett reached over Logan's shoulder and fouled him. Garrett swore and the Jefferson rooters cheered.

"You, you, you!" they said, pointing at Garrett.

The Patriots' bench stood and raised their arms.

"All right, Eddie!" Cisco shouted, clapping.

"What a sub!," Brian said, laughing. "Hey, Garrett, what happened?"

When Brian returned to the game with his four fouls, Eddie Logan had scored four points and had grabbed two rebounds. He also had made Garrett more tired.

The Patriots' fans gave him a standing ovation.

Eddie trotted to the bench with four minutes to play and the score tied 66–66. The championship was still up for grabs, and both teams were like tired boxers at the end of a long fight.

"Watch out, homeboy," LaMont told Brian as he ran to play defense, "we don't wanna lose you on fouls."

"I'm gonna play hard," Brian said. "We can't lose to these Quiller punks."

Butler's fieldhouse was rocking with cheers. Brian could feel the tension in the air.

Drew dribbled across midcourt and set up Quiller's offense. The Chargers' starters were breathing hard from exhaustion. Their navy blue jerseys were soaked with sweat.

Garrett faked to the free-throw line, then cut to the basket for a lob pass by Drew. Garrett was tired and he reached the pass a little late. Brian leaped and stole the ball.

"Davis!" Reggie shouted, sprinting downcourt ahead of Drew, who looked dead on his feet.

Brian whipped a length-of-the-court baseball pass to Reggie, who dribbled twice and slam-dunked the ball through the hoop.

The score was Jefferson 68 and Quiller 66.

The happy Patriot subs jumped off the bench, their fists raised.

In the Chargers' court, Garrett cut to the free-throw line and Brian slammed into a pick by Dishman. While Brian struggled to step around Dishman, Drew passed to Garrett, who started to shoot a jumper from fifteen feet.

"Fight through the pick!" LaMont shouted at Brian.

Dishman tried to hold Brian's jersey, but he smacked his hand away and leaped toward Garrett.

Brian timed his jump perfectly and blocked the shot.

The Jefferson rooters stood and cheered, but Garrett pushed several players away and grabbed the loose ball. He turned, and without faking tried another jumper from near the base line.

Brian stayed with Garrett and blocked his second try.

After watching two blocked shots in a row, the fans in the fieldhouse went crazy.

But Garrett wasn't finished. He grabbed the ball as soon as Brian blocked it and tried a jump shot from ten feet away. Brian timed his leap again, and for the third time in ten seconds blocked Garrett's shot.

The fieldhouse erupted with a loud roar.

"Three blocks in a row!" Coach Williams shouted from the Patriots' bench. He leaped to his feet along with the subs and cheered.

Terry picked up the loose ball, passed it down-court to LaMont, who laid it in over a tired Dishman.

The score was 70 to 66, and Quiller looked beaten.

The final two minutes of the game belonged to the Patriots. They dribbled away from the exhausted Chargers and ate up the most of the remaining time on the clock.

The Jefferson fans called out the final seconds. *"Five, four, three, two, one!"*

The final score was Patriots 72, Quiller 70.

Brian and his teammates were mobbed on the court by their happy rooters.

LaMont grabbed Brian in a bear hug as their fans patted them on the back.

"We're sectional champs!" Reggie shouted jumping up and down. "We're the champs!"

NINE

"Brian Davis, sectional tourney MVP," Tony said as he walked along a sidewalk with Brian and Reggie.

"Davis deserved it," Reggie said, bouncing his basketball as they walked. "Man, thirty points and twenty-one rebounds! That's what an MVP is supposed to do."

"And what about the blocked shots?" Tony said, looking up at Brian. "*Ten* of 'em, and three in a row against Garrett."

"You guys make me sound like Superman," Brian said, a bit embarrassed by all the attention.

"Man, you are!" Reggie said, nudging Brian playfully.

Tony nodded. "Even the sportswriters said so in this morning's paper," the bushy-haired junior said.

"Yeah, Davis, they said they'd never seen anybody take over a game like you did in the fourth quarter last night," Reggie added. "Man, what a show."

It was early afternoon on the Sunday after the Patriots won the sectional championship. Brian and his two best friends were walking to the nearby park to play a few games of H-O-R-S-E. It was hard to stop playing ball, even after such a tough game as the final against Quiller.

"You did okay, Dupree," Brian said as they crossed the street and headed for the park's asphalt courts.

"Yeah, Reg, you made the All-Sectional team," Tony added. "That ain't too shabby."

"LaMont should've made it, too," Reggie said as they stepped through a hole in the battered chain-link fence and walked onto the outdoor courts. "Dude played good ball."

Brian warmed his hands by blowing on them and shot a few times at the rusty rim. It was chilly on the courts. The three Patriots shot around for a while, then played a few games of H-O-R-S-E, which Brian won easily.

"Man, give us a break, Davis," Reggie said, smiling.

"Yeah, you ain't the MVP here," Tony said, "so let us scrubs win a game or two."

Brian laughed, and it felt good to be a Patriot and a sectional champ. Then he saw Mo Gernert and Mickey Wright walking toward them, and his happy feeling evaporated.

"Hey," Tony said, "ain't that . . . ?"

"Yeah, it is," Brian asked, trying to ignore the nervous lump in his stomach.

"Hi, boys," Gernert said, smiling and shaking hands with all three of them.

"You all know Mickey," Gernert said, gesturing at the unsmiling Wright. "Mick's an old playground player, too."

"Yeah, great game last night," Wright said dully, not changing his steely expression.

Wright glared at Brian.

"Could you guys give Brian and me a few moments to talk in private?" Gernert said, smiling.

Brian exchanged glances with Reggie and Tony.

"Ah, maybe I shouldn't," Brian said, licking his lips.

"Come on, it's no big deal," Wright said, grabbing Brian's arm and edging him toward the car. "We'll be back."

As Brian walked toward Gernert's white Cadillac, he glanced over his shoulder and saw worried looks on his two teammates' faces. With his heart pounding, Brian got into the backseat with Wright and Gernert drove away.

"You know the K and M Cafeteria on the Northside?" Gernert asked Brian as they drove past Jefferson High.

"Yeah," Brian said, trying to stay calm.

"I figured you'd feel more like talking if we went to a place you know," Gernert said, smiling.

They arrived at the cafeteria, which was half-empty now that most of the Sunday dinner crowd had left. Brian followed Gernert and Wright to a quiet table at the rear of the large dining room.

Gernert looked at Brian and got right to the point of the meeting.

"I got a deal for you, Brian," Gernert said, smiling and looking as harmless as somebody's friendly uncle.

"A deal?" Brian said, looking at Wright, who still was hard faced.

"A financial deal," Gernert said, "a way for you to help your mom with all the bills she has to pay."

"I don't understand," Brian said.

"It's simple," Gernert continued, "you do something for me and I'll pay you handsomely for it."

"Yeah, man," Wright said in his dull voice, "Mo's money's the best. Nobody pays more."

"We're talking about one thousand dollars to start," Gernert told Brian, smiling warmly. "How's that sound?"

"One thousand . . . dollars?" Brian said, looking from Gernert to Wright, then back again. "It's . . . great."

"What did I tell you, Mick," Gernert said, nodding at Wright. "The kid knows a good deal when he sees it."

"What do I gotta do?" Brian asked, still nervous.

Brian watched as Gernert looked around the cafeteria, then adjusted his glasses and leaned closer to him.

"Just miss a few jump shots or lay-ups in Saturday's game against Morris North, that's all," Gernert said.

Gernert's words struck Brian like a slap in the face.

"You mean . . . throw the game?" Brian said, his heart in his throat.

"Naw, man, just make the score different, you know?" Wright said, speaking as normally as if they were discussing Brian's history homework. "You ain't gonna lose the game or nothing. Just fix the point spread, that's all."

"But that's . . . against the law," Brian said.

Gernert and Wright laughed, then Gernert leaned close to Brian again.

"Nobody's gonna know about it," he said, smiling.

"I did it for years," Wright said, "in high school and later in college. It's easy, man."

"And you and your mom sure can use the money," Gernert repeated. "We'll start you out at a thousand bucks, and if you do good, we'll raise it to three or four thousand for big games like the finals."

Brian's head was spinning, and he couldn't believe his ears. He swallowed and looked at Gernert.

"I . . . I can't," Brian said. "It ain't right."

Gernert and Wright exchanged a glance, then Gernert grabbed Brian's right hand so hard it hurt.

"Listen, we're not *asking* you to do this," the slick dressing hustler said, "we're telling you."

Gernert squeezed Brian's shooting hand even harder.

"If you tell anybody about this conversation or don't do what we want, I'll let Mick bust you up so bad you won't play ball again. Is that clear, Brian?"

Suddenly Gernert didn't sound like a friendly uncle.

Brian nodded and was glad when Gernert released his shooting hand.

"Why . . . why me?" Brian said, rubbing his hand.

"Because I figure Jefferson High's gonna go far in the tournament," Gernert said, "and without a good backup center to give you a blow once in a while, you'll be playing a lot. And you'll be able to do what we want."

"Great deal, eh, man?" Wright said, laughing coldly.

Brian didn't answer, but just got up and followed Gernert and Wright out of the cafeteria.

"Don't forget," Gernert told Brian as he stopped his Cadillac near the outdoor courts where Reggie and Tony were still shooting hoops, "keep the score of Saturday's Morris North game in the sixties and there'll be a thousand dollars for you. And that's the beginning, son."

Gernert winked at Brian, who got out of the car.

"We'll check back with you before Saturday's game," Gernert said through his rolled-down window.

The fast-talking game fixer drove away.

"What happened?" Tony said, walking to where Brian stood watching the Cadillac disappear around a corner.

Brian looked at his teammates and found he was so scared he was shaking.

"I . . . I can't tell you," Brian said, walking out of the park. "Believe me, I can't say anything."

"Davis?" Reggie asked, stepping up behind him.

"I gotta go home," Brian said, waving to his friends over his shoulder and almost running from the park.

TEN

After a restless night, Brian awoke on Monday and decided he had to tell somebody about Gernert's offer.

"Say what?" Reggie asked after Brian told Tony and him what had happened at the K and M Cafeteria on their way to school.

"Wow, that's heavy," Tony said, shaking his head.

"What are you going to do?" Reggie asked Brian. "This Gernert dude sounds like trouble."

"Yeah, both him and Wright look like gangsters," Tony added. "You need help."

"Maybe I oughta tell Coach Ford," Brian said as they walked closer to Jefferson High.

"What could he do?" Reggie asked.

"yeah, he'd just go to the cops," Tony said. "Then Gernert would really be ticked off at you."

"This whole thing's about the Patriots," Brian

said, "so I figure Coach Ford oughta know about it."

"That's cool," Reggie said, "but do me a favor and tell him this morning. I don't want some dudes busting into the gym during practice and machine-gunning everybody."

"Dupree, you got a big imagination," Brian said, but Reggie's words sent a chill through him, anyway.

The three teammates walked to Coach Ford's office before classes began and Brian told him everything.

When Brian finished, Coach Ford stared at him.

"Well, what do we do, Coach?" Brian asked finally.

"I've heard about Gernert," Coach Ford said, "but I never figured he'd approach one of my players."

"The dude sounds serious," Reggie said, looking nervous, as if he were still thinking about machine guns.

"He is," Coach Ford said, reaching for his telephone. "Gernert's been in jail a few times for this same thing."

"Are you gonna call the police?" Brian asked.

"Yeah, and the FBI, too," the coach said, checking the phone directory for numbers. "They'll tell us what to do."

"Man, the FBI," Reggie said, his eyes wide.

"Whatever you three do," Coach Ford added, "don't mention this to anybody else here at school until we meet with the law-enforcement people."

The school day passed slowly for Brian, until finally he was called to the office after lunch. Waiting in Mr. Rhodes's office were the principal,

Coach Ford, and two serious-looking men dressed in suits. Mr. Rhodes introduced the men as FBI agents Walker and Sanderson.

"We've heard the details of your story, Brian," said Agent Walker, a middle-aged bald man, "and we'd like you to help us catch Gernert. You know, put him out of business."

"Me?" Brian asked, swallowing hard. "H— How?"

"Gernert said he'd check back with you," said Agent Sanderson, who wore a crew cut and looked too young to be a FBI man, "so we'd like to set a trap for him."

"With me as the . . . bait?" Brian asked.

Mr. Rhodes and Coach Ford laughed, but the two agents kept their serious expressions.

"Not really, Brian," Agent Walker said, running a hand over his bald head. "We'll have a team of agents watching you all week, just in case."

"You won't see the men," Agent Sanderson added, "but they'll be around in case Gernert shows up."

"You mean I'm gonna be followed?" Brian asked.

"In a manner of speaking, yes," Agent Walker said.

"Brian, we feel it's the only way to get this Gernert off the streets for good," Coach Ford said.

"And we want him to stop bothering you, too," said Mr. Rhodes, smiling at Brian.

"Gernert's testing you," Agent Walker said. "If he likes the way you fix games, he'll keep on using you."

"We've seen this pattern before," Agent Sanderson added. "That's why we want to get him before he strings you along too far."

Brian took a deep breath, then nodded.

"Okay, all I want to do is play ball," he said, looking at the two FBI men. "I'll do whatever you want."

"I don't think Gernert'll pull a gun or anything like that," Agent Walker said, standing now near the door, "so you shouldn't be in danger."

Suddenly Brian pictured Gernert and Wright running after him, big machine guns drawn. He forced the thought from his mind and looked up at Agent Walker again.

"Can I tell my mom and aunt about this?" he asked.

He watched the FBI agents exchange glances with Coach Ford and Mr. Rhodes.

"I'll explain the situation to your mom today," Coach Ford said. "I'm sure she'll understand."

Brian's mom and aunt were shocked when they learned about Gernert, and for Brian the rest of the week was full of tension and the worry of what might happen to him.

"Work on your defense," Coach Ford kept telling the Patriots for the first three days of practice. Brian tried to keep his mind on basketball, but it was hard.

The Morris North Bulldogs were going to be the Patriots' opponents at twelve-thirty in the afternoon during Saturday's regional tourney at Butler's fieldhouse. The Bulldogs had upset favored Lincoln North in their sectional.

The Westside Lions, with their powerful center

Oscar Brown, would play the scrappy Pyle High Packers during the first game at eleven o'clock. The winners of the two games were scheduled to play for the regional championship Saturday night at eight o'clock. The Patriots were psyched.

"Morris North is tough," Coach Williams told Brian and the Patriots over and over. "Stay hungry."

"There are only sixty-four teams left in the tournament," Coach Ford reminded the team. "All of 'em are good."

"Yeah, but we're the best," Terry said, clapping his hands as Wednesday's practice ended.

At Thursday's practice, several TV crews taped interviews with Brian, Reggie, and Coach Ford. For Brian, the unresolved Gernert situation made it hard to concentrate on the announcers' questions during the long session.

"I'm not giving any more interviews," Tony said after Brian finished. "Those TV dudes never used my other one so they'll just have to eat their hearts out from now on."

The Patriots playfully tossed basketballs at Zarella, but Brian found it hard to have fun.

After practice, Brian changed clothes and headed home through the early-March darkness. As he'd done all week, he looked around for Agent Walker's FBI men, but as usual he couldn't see any.

Two blocks from his aunt's house, he turned as a car approached from behind. It was Gernert's white Cadillac.

Brian felt a stab of fear in his stomach.

He tried to act normally and not look around for the FBI, but felt sure he was giving the agents away by acting like a nervous rookie. He took a deep breath to calm himself.

"Hi, Brian," Gernert said through the window on the driver's side. "Looking forward to Saturday's game?"

"Uh . . . yeah, sure," Brian said, trying to swallow but unable to. His pulse began to pound in his throat as Gernert and Wright got out of the Caddie and stepped over to him.

"Our deal still on?" Gernert said, adjusting his wire-rimmed glasses and smiling up at Brian. He looked like somebody's friendly uncle again. Wright was still hard faced.

"Ah, yeah," Brian said, trying to smile but wondering where the FBI agents were. He saw Wright staring at him.

"Just to be sure," Gernert said, reaching into a jacket pocket and pulling out a wad of hundred-dollar bills, "I want to give you a little advance. You know, to show I'm a good guy."

Gernert counted out five bills and handed them to Brian. Suddenly the bushes all around them rustled and FBI men rushed Brian and the two game fixers.

"Don't move!" Agent Walker shouted, a gun in his hand.

Brian's heart skipped a beat when he saw the gun.

Gernert acted quickly and shoved Mickey Wright into Agent Walker. Then he grabbed Brian by the arms and used him as a shield. He backed toward his white Cadillac.

"Stupid kid!" Gernert shouted, pushing Brian aside as he dived into his Caddie.

The big car's engine roared to life, and Gernert

sped away down the street. The Caddie's tires squealed as it raced around a corner and disappeared.

Brian stood on wobbly legs and gasped for air.

"You okay?" Agent Walker asked, running over to him.

Brian could barely catch his breath, but he nodded and watched as the other agents handcuffed Wright and led him to a car.

"Gernert got away," Brian said finally.

He handed the five bills to Agent Walker.

"Don't worry, we'll catch up to him," said the young agent Sanderson as he joined them.

"I don't think we'll see Gernert around here again," Agent Walker said as he holstered his gun. He patted Brian on the back. "Not with kids like you who stand up to him."

And that was goods news for Brian, who breathed deeply and finally felt he could think about the regional again.

ELEVEN

"Go, Patriots, go! Go, Patriots, go!"

Waving red-white-and-blue pom-poms, Jefferson High's cheerleaders yelled and did splits along the sidelines of Butler University's sixty-year-old fieldhouse.

In the bleacher-type seats, almost fifteen thousand fans clapped and waited for the start of the regional tournament's second game. At eleven in the morning, Pyle High had upset Westside in overtime to win the first game.

"A crowd this size gets me psyched," LaMont told Brian as the Patriots warmed up for their twelve-thirty game against Morris North.

"Man, I don't need a crowd to get me psyched," Reggie said, shooting a jumper. "I wanna play in the finals tonight. We gonna go all the way this year, I can feel it."

"Yeah, but like Coach says," Brian told Reggie, "let's win 'em one at a time."

"That's cool," Reggie said, "but I wanna play against Pyle. Man, can you believe they beat Westside?"

"Maybe you don't want to play 'em, Dupree," Brian said. "They looked tough."

"We gotta win this Morris North game now," Tony said, dribbling over. "Then the finals game tonight."

"I'm beat just thinking about it," Brian said, swishing a long jump shot.

"Yeah, Davis has played almost every minute since the tourney started," Reggie said. "Dude's gotta be wiped out."

"Let's just think about the game," LaMont reminded his teammates. He glanced at the other end of the court where the Morris North Bulldogs, dressed in red-and-black uniforms, were warming up.

"There's Reynaldo Nance," Reggie said as he and Brian huddled near midcourt with LaMont. Clarence Reed dribbled over and pulled his goggles onto his forehead.

"Like Coach told us," LaMont said, "Nance can really bury those three-pointers. Dude's been the best outside shooter in the city this season. Don't give him time to put 'em up."

"That Wilkerson dude looks big," Clarence said, pointing at North's six-foot-ten center.

"Yeah, but Coach says he's slow," Terry said, joining them. "Davis oughta leave him in the dust."

"He ain't that bad," Brian said, bouncing his ball. "He out-played Dexter Cole in the sectional, and Cole scored over thirty points against us."

"The rest of 'em are nothing," Brian said, "but we better not get sloppy."

"Yeah, guys," LaMont said, turning and leading them back to their warm-ups, "this is the regional and it's no place for dudes who don't put out all the time."

"Don't worry, bro," Reggie said, swishing a long jump shot, "we gonna kick butt today."

"Yeah, twice," Terry added. "Now, and tonight."

"All right!" Clarence said, bashing forearms with Terry and Reggie.

The buzzer sounded, the fans cheered, and the players ran to their benches. After the introduction of both starting fives, the teams huddled around their coaches.

"After today," Coach Ford shouted over the loud music of the Eastside High pep band, "there'll be only sixteen teams left in the tournament. Let's be one of 'em."

"Yeah, all right!" shouted several players.

Brian and the usual starting lineup, dressed in their white uniforms, walked to the midcourt jump-ball circle.

"Think you can out-jump Wilkerson?" LaMont asked Brian. "Dude doesn't look like he can jump."

"Yeah, tap the ball to Jackson," Reggie said. "I'm taking off downcourt."

"Okay, let's do a play," Brian said.

The refs checked with the timer and scorer, and the players shook hands. The fans from both schools were yelling. Brian felt the tension in the air.

The ref tossed up the ball, and Brian won the jump, tapping the ball toward LaMont. But North's six-two black guard, Reynaldo Nance, stepped in and stole it.

Reggie ran back from downcourt.

The Morris North cheering section waved black-and-red pom-poms and cheered wildly. Coach Ford shouted orders.

"Get back on defense," LaMont told the Patriots.

"I got Nance," Reggie said. He crouched into a guarding stance and looked at North's top scorer. "Come on, baby, show me that long bomb of yours."

Brian guarded Bob Wilkerson and watched as Nance tricky-dribbled around Reggie, then stopped and shot a long jumper from beyond the three-point arc.

The high-arching shot touched nothing but net as it swished through.

Morris North led 3–0, and their fans cheered.

"Don't let the dude shoot from there," LaMont told Reggie as they ran downcourt to set up the offense.

"Man, the guy's tricky," Reggie said.

The Patriots crossed the midcourt line.

"They're playing zone!" Terry shouted as he dribbled at the top of the key. "Set up the plays."

Brian ran along the base line looking for a lob pass. Wilkerson, playing in the rear of North's zone, kept an eye on him. Near the key, Nance pressured Terry.

"Hanson!" LaMont shouted, raising his hand and cutting toward the foul lane.

Rushing a little, Terry tried a quick overhead pass. Russ Oliver, North's alert five-ten playmaker, slapped the ball away when it was behind Hanson's head and batted it to Reynaldo Nance.

The Morris North Bulldogs started a fast break.

"Get back!" LaMont shouted, running after Nance.

But before Brian and the other Patriots could recover, the six-two Nance dribbled alone to the hoop and slam-dunked the ball. North now led 5–0.

The fieldhouse rocked with the cheers of the Morris North fans.

"Take care of the ball," Brian told Terry. "Watch out for their double teams."

"Cut through their zone and I'll hit you with a pass," Terry shouted to Brian as they ran back downcourt.

The Patriots set up their zone offense and Brian suddenly noticed Wilkerson was late getting back on defense.

"Hanson!" Brian shouted, raising his hand and cutting to the hoop.

The Morris North coach yelled and pointed at Brian.

But Wilkerson recovered too late. Terry lobbed an alley-oop pass that Brian caught with both hands and slammed down through the basket. The score was now 5–2.

Finally, the Patriots' fans had a reason to cheer.

"Nice pass," Brian told Terry, bashing forearms.

North inbounded the ball, and Russ Oliver dribbled over the ten-second line and looked for Nance. Wilkerson cut and positioned himself behind Reggie.

"Dupree, watch the pick!" Brian shouted, but his warning came too late.

Reggie, trying to stick close to Nance, slammed into the solid pick by Wilkerson. Brian didn't switch out in time and Oliver whipped a chest pass to Nance, who swished another three-pointer. The score was now North 8 and the Patriots 2.

"You guys gotta switch on that," Coach Ford shouted from the bench. "Play tougher D."

"You okay?" Brian asked Reggie, who was shaking his head. "You hit that pick pretty good."

"Yeah, it felt like a brick wall," Reggie said.

"Look for good shots," LaMont said as the Patriots ran downcourt. "Work the ball against the zone."

Terry and Reggie passed the ball around in front of North's slow-moving zone until LaMont broke free near the foul lane. Reggie looked one way, then fired a chest pass to LaMont, who was quickly guarded by two Bulldogs.

Brian saw Wilkerson rush over to LaMont, so he cut to the basket and raised his hand. LaMont up-faked once and passed to Brian, who turned and swished a short jump shot.

"*Da-vis! Da-vis!*" shouted the Patriots' cheer-leaders.

"Way to shoot, homeboy," Clarence said, bashing forearms. "Let's stop 'em on defense."

"Give me some help with Nance," Reggie said, getting ready to chase the Bulldogs' sharpshooter.

But the Patriots had trouble with Reynaldo Nance for the rest of the first quarter. He used picks by Wilkerson to get open in the corners and swished two more three-point bombs.

"Whoosh!" shouted North's fans on every successful three-pointer by Nance.

For the Patriots, the lumbering Wilkerson was no match for Brian. Brian shot over and around the six-ten giant and was Jefferson's only offense in the first period.

But thanks to North's fast start, they led at the end of one quarter, 22–18.

"We gotta stop Nance," Coach Ford shouted as the Patriots huddled near their bench. "Give Dupree some help with him."

"Maybe we can double-team the dude," LaMont said, toweling off.

"Yeah, how about me and Reg taking Nance and everybody else covering their men?" Terry said.

"That's cool," Coach Williams said in his deep voice, "but Davis has gotta stay near the hoop to stop 'em if somebody gets free for a pass from Nance."

"Sorta like a goalkeeper?" Brian asked, tossing his towel onto the bench.

"That's right," Coach Ford said. "Swat everything back at 'em."

The Patriots walked back onto the court and Clarence tossed the ball into Terry to start the second quarter. The North Bulldogs were still playing a two-three zone defense. Both teams kept their starters in the game.

"Work the ball around the zone," LaMont shouted.

Suddenly Nance and Oliver double-teamed Terry. Reggie was open and yelled for a pass.

Terry leaped and whipped an overhead pass above the arms of the two North guards. Reggie caught the call outside the three-point line and swished a twenty-two-footer.

"Whoosh!" shouted the Patriots' fans.

The score was now North 22 and Jefferson 21.

"Keep it up, Dupree," Brian said as he ran past Reggie. "Make 'em pay for that double team."

At North's end of the floor, Nance didn't hesitate.

The six-two guard dribbled to the top of the three-point arc and launched a high-arching bomb that swished through the basket.

"Whoosh!" yelled North's fans, waving their pom-poms.

"Where's our double team?" Coach Ford shouted.

As the quarter wound down, Reggie and Nance traded long bombs again. But when the defenses of both teams finally smothered their outside shots, big players like Brian and Wilkerson were suddenly open for moves closer to the hoop.

"Dupree!" Brian shouted near the end of the half.

Reggie, being double-teamed by Nance and Oliver, whipped a hook pass to Brian in the foul lane. Brian caught the bullet pass, faked Wilkerson off his feet, and made a short jumper.

At North's end of the court, Reggie and Terry double-teamed Nance and stopped his three-point shot. But the six-two bomber passed to Wilkerson in the lane. The center faked Brian with a quick ball feint, then swished a short jumper over his head.

With the score tied and the fans counting off the final second of the second quarter, Brian caught a long pass from Reggie near the top of the key. He turned to face the basket.

"Shoot, Davis!" shouted Tony from the bench.

Brian launched a thirty-foot jumper as the buzzer ending the first half sounded. The ball swished through the hoop for a three-pointer. The fans went wild.

"All right!" shouted several Patriots' subs, running across the floor toward the downstairs locker room.

The score at half time was Jefferson 41 and the Morris North Bulldogs 38.

Reggie opened the third quarter by raising his hand in the left corner. Brian, double-teamed under the hoop by Wilkerson and a North forward, whipped a pass to Dupree.

Reggie swished a three-point jumper.

"Whoosh!" shouted the Jefferson rooters.

Nance answered for the Bulldogs by racing downcourt, stopping on a dime at the right side of the key, and making a twenty-footer with Reggie and Terry all over him.

At the end of three quarters, both teams were exhausted. The score was tied, 58–58.

"This is it, guys," LaMont told the Patriots on the bench between periods. "One quarter to win the game."

"Yeah, and then the finals tonight," Terry said.

"Man, we can do it," Reggie shouted, bashing forearms with everybody.

The teams, their uniforms soaked with sweat, walked onto the court to start the final eight minutes. The fans from both schools rocked the fieldhouse with their cheers.

Brian felt the excitement all around him.

"Come on, homeboy," Clarence said, adjusting his goggles, "give us one of your super quarters."

Brian took a deep breath and nodded. He was used to being the player everybody counted on.

North opened the final quarter by passing the ball in to Russ Oliver. The Bulldogs' playmaker dribbled across the ten-second line and looked for

Nance, who was being hounded by Reggie. Suddenly, Nance set a pick for Wilkerson.

"Watch out!" Reggie shouted at Brian.

But Nance held his ground and Brian nearly ran over him. Wilkerson cut free and now was guarded by Reggie.

Oliver passed the ball to Wilkerson, who turned and shot a short jumper.

Brian fought around the pick by the smaller Nance. Stretching his six-eight frame to its full height, he blocked the shot as it left Wilkerson's hand. Reggie picked up the loose ball and started a fast break.

The Patriots' fans stood and cheered.

Reggie stopped at the free-throw line, looked at his closely guarded teammates, and shot a jumper.

The ball bounced off the back of the rim and into the air. Wilkerson, LaMont, and another North forward tried to grab the rebound. Brian leaped into the lane and beat them to it.

"Davis!" Reggie shouted, raising his hand and running beyond the three-point circle.

Brian whipped a chest pass to Reggie, who calmly swished another three-point jump shot.

The fans cheered, and for the first time Brian saw looks of defeat on the faces of the Morris North Bulldogs. For the rest of the quarter, the Patriots dominated North on both offense and defense. The fans sensed victory and stayed on their feet, cheering and waving pom-poms.

With twenty seconds left to play, Jefferson led 80 to 77. Wilkerson tried a jump shot, but Brian blocked it back into the center's face. Nance picked up the loose ball and tried a ten-foot jump shot from the lane, but Brian leaped and blocked *his* shot, too.

Reggie grabbed the ball and dribbled for the final few seconds. The Patriots' fans counted as the clock wound down.

"*Three, two, one!*" they shouted, running onto the court and engulfing the Patriot players.

The final score was Jefferson 80 and North 77.

Brian finished the game with 35 points, 18 rebounds, and seven blocked shots. Reggie scored 33 points, including eight three-pointers. Nance had 36 points for Morris North, including a Regional record eleven three-pointers.

After the fans finally left the floor, Nance walked over to Brian.

"Good game, man," said the Bulldogs' star. "And good luck tonight against Pyle."

Brian shook hands and nodded. "Thanks. We'll need it."

TWELVE

"Man, I'm tired," Reggie said, munching on a bologna sandwich.

"We ain't got time to be tired," LaMont said, taking a swig from a Gatorade bottle.

"Yeah," Terry said, checking his watch, "there are only four hours more until the final game starts."

"That's plenty of time for Dupree to do some of Coach Mel's defense drills," Brian said, smiling at Reggie.

The Patriots laughed and continued their lunch.

Brian and his teammates were eating bag lunches in the Jefferson High gym and resting for that evening's championship game against the Pyle High Packers. It was the first time that season the Patriots would have to play two games in one day.

"Okay, listen up," Coach Ford said, walking into

the gym from his office. "Here's the scoop on Pyle."

B-team coach Pat Young, the Patriots' scout followed Coaches Ford and Williams. Brian and his teammates finished eating.

"Pyle may be the best team we've played all season," Coach Young said, adjusting his thick-rimmed glasses.

"Man, better than Gary Tech! And Westside?" Reggie asked, a surprised look on his face.

"Pyle beat Westside this morning," Coach Williams said stroking his goatee, "and they held Oscar Brown, one of the state's best centers, to eleven points."

Brian saw some anxious looks on the players' faces.

"Pyle's best player is their six-six black center, Wilbur Carrington," Coach Young continued.

"Dude's good," Clarence said, chewing the last of his sandwich. "Plays downtown and eats up a lot of guys with his defense."

"He ain't bad on the boards, neither," LaMont said.

"He's yours, Davis," Coach Ford said.

"Have fun, man," Reggie said, bashing forearms with Brain.

"Pyle's also got a six-five white power forward they call 'Bull' Howard," Coach Ford said, looking up from his clipboard and smiling at the players.

Brian and the Patriots laughed at the nickname.

"He's a good player," Coach Ford said, "so don't laugh too hard. You gotta keep him off the boards."

"Yeah," Terry said, laughing, "Bull must be an animal under the hoop."

The Patriots laughed again, then returned their attention to Coach Young.

"Finally, their six-three white guard, Alex Hall, is one of the best short-range jump shooters around," said the B-team coach, adjusting his glasses. "Good passer, too."

"Don't forget about Marty LaRue," Coach Ford said. "The kid's a specialist on defense."

Coach Young nodded. "He's got quick hands," he said.

"Dude's gotta prove it to me," Reggie said.

"Well, that's it," Coach Ford said, looking at the players. "The rest is up to you guys. Remember there'll only be sixteen teams left in the tournament after tonight."

"Let's be one of 'em," LaMont said.

"All right!" shouted Cisco Vega and several other players, clapping their hands

"We're goin' all the way to Market Square Arena!" Terry said, bashing forearms with his teammates.

Later that evening, as the Patriots ran onto the court for their warm-ups, the tension in the Butler fieldhouse was so real Brian could feel it all around him.

More than fifteen thousand fans were shouting.

"Man, I'm ready," Reggie said in the lay-up line.

"Me, too," Brian said, looking down at the Pyle Packers, dressed in black uniforms, "but so are those guys."

"We'll take 'em," Terry said, running in for a shot.

After warming up, both teams were introduced

to the big crowd, then huddled with their coaches.

"I know you're tired," Coach Ford said over the noise echoing in the hangarlike fieldhouse, "but go as hard as you can."

"Pyle's tired, too," Coach Williams added.

"This is a championship game," Coach Ford continued, "so you gotta play with something extra."

The Patriots huddled and shouted, "Let's go!" Then the usual starters walked to midcourt for the jump ball.

Brian's legs felt tired, but he ignored them.

Wilbur Carrington stepped into the jump-ball circle, and Brian shook the six-six center's hand.

"You guys're no better than Westside," Carrington said, scowling at Brian. "We gonna whip you, too."

"Talk is cheap," Brian said. "Show me what you got."

The fans cheered wildly, the timer nodded that he was ready, and the ref tossed up the ball to start the regional final. Brian leaped as high as his tired legs would let him, but Carrington won the jump and tapped the ball to Pyle's six-three guard, Alex Hall.

"Pick 'em up," LaMont shouted over the cheers of the Packers' fans.

Brian ran downcourt alongside Carrington, who immediately started elbowing him in the side.

Hall dribbled near the top of the key, with Reggie in his shirt. The other Packers cut around and through Jefferson's tight man-to-man defense. Brian stayed close to Carrington.

Suddenly, Bull Howard set a pick on Brian, and Carrington cut to the hoop. Clarence was caught off guard and didn't switch to stop Carrington near the basket.

Hall whipped a pass to Carrington, who slam-dunked the ball.

The Pyle rooters stood and waved black-and white pom-poms. Carrington raised his fist and ran downcourt to play defense.

"You gotta talk on defense," Coach Ford yelled as Brian and the Patriots ran past to set up their offense.

Brian set up along the base line against Carrington, who shoved and elbowed him in the back. Terry dribbled to the right side of the court and tried to pass the ball to Reggie back at the free-throw line. Marty LaRue, the Packers' six-one white guard, leaped and stole the pass.

"Get back!" LaMont shouted, but it was too late.

LaRue dribbled quickly downcourt and passed the ball to Carrington, who ran around Brian and dunked the ball again.

The score was Pyle 4 and Jefferson 0, and the fieldhouse erupted with cheers.

"Come on, guys," Terry said, dribbling back downcourt. "Now it's our turn."

Brian set up again along the base line, and almost immediately Terry whipped a chest pass that sneaked past Carrington's outstretched hand. Brian turned and stepped to the hoop—but Carrington blocked his shot from behind.

Alex Hall picked up the loose ball and raced downcourt. With Reggie on his heels, Hall drove to the hoop and laid in a reverse lay-up. Reggie tried to block the shot but smacked Hall for a foul as the ball swished through the net.

Hall made the free throw, and the Pyle fans

rocked the fieldhouse with cheers. The score was 7 to 0.

Back at the Patriots' end of the court, Reggie tried a long jumper but Marty LaRue bothered him into shooting an air ball. Carrington out-jumped Brian and Clarence, then grabbed the ball and fired an outlet pass to Hall.

"*Air ball, air ball!*" yelled the Pyle fans at Reggie.

The Packers raced down the floor again, but this time Alex Hall stopped and swished a fifteen-foot jumper.

The score was now Pyle 9 and Jefferson 0, and Coach Ford called a time-out.

The Packer fans stood and cheered their team.

"Man, we look sick," Reggie said, toweling off on the Patriots' bench.

"These dudes aren't *this* good," LaMont said, slumping next to Brian.

"Keep your cool, guys," Coach Ford shouted over the music and cheers. "We've dug ourselves a hole and it'll take awhile to get back in the game."

The Patriots inbounded the ball, and finally Terry got the ball to Brian near the hoop. Brian swished a jumper over Carrington, breaking the Patriots' scoring drought.

The teams traded hoops for the rest of the first quarter. Carrington scored on two jumpers and Hall hit a long jumper. Reggie and Terry were hounded by the close guarding of LaRue and Hall. Brian managed to swish another jumper against Carrington, while Clarence and LaMont scored on tip-ins of missed shots.

The score at the end of the first quarter was Pyle 15 and Jefferson 11.

Reggie and Terry had made a combined total of one basket in eight tries against Marty LaRue's defense.

"Keep trying, Reg," Brian said, toweling off between quarters. "Don't let 'em get you down."

But Coach Ford sent Alvin in for Reggie to start the second quarter. Pyle's lineup remained the same.

"Work the plays," LaMont said. "Set good picks."

Clarence inbounded the ball to Terry to begin the quarter. LaMont picked off Marty LaRue for the first time, and Alvin was free for a pass and a fifteen-foot jump shot. The five-eight sophomore made the basket, and Jefferson's fans had something good to cheer about.

In the middle of the quarter, Brian guarded Carrington closely as the Pyle center tried a short jumper. He slapped Carrington's arm for a foul as he swished the shot, then felt a sharp pain in his left calf. It felt like somebody was sticking a knife in his leg, and he fell to the floor and grabbed his calf.

The refs called Coach Ford onto the court.

"You okay, Davis?" Clarence asked. The Patriots' fans were holding their breath in the bleachers.

Brian held on to his leg and looked up at Coach Ford. His calf felt like it was tied in knots.

"Looks like a cramp," the coach said, rubbing Brian's calf. "This happens a lot when you play two games on the same day."

Brain finally felt better, but Coach Ford took him out of the game for a brief rest.

Eddie Logan checked in at center.

"Stay with Carrington," Brian told Eddie as he walked past. "Block him away from the boards."

But the skinny freshman was no match for Carrington. Pyle's senior center scored twice on lay-ups, then tipped in a missed shot by Hall. On offense, Eddie missed two short jumpers and a pair of free throws after Carrington pushed him to the floor. Pyle built up a lead.

Brian stayed on the bench for the rest of the second quarter, and at half time the score was Pyle 33 and the Patriots 25.

Brian's leg cramp disappeared at half time, and he opened the third quarter with the usual starting lineup. The Packers' same lineup also returned, and the game immediately became a battle under the hoop between Brian and Carrington.

On offense, Brian started driving to the hoop against Carrington, who fouled him twice. Brian swished four free throws during the quarter, and also made a fifteen-foot jump shot over Carrington's long arms. Reggie, Terry, and Alvin continued to shoot poorly against Marty LaRue, the Packers' defensive specialist.

On defense, Brian made Carrington work hard for everything, including passes from Hall. Carrington scored only on offensive rebounds after some missed shots by the other Packers, and along with Bull Howard controlled the rebounding.

The third quarter ended with Pyle leading 49–42.

"Okay," Coach Ford shouted over the noise in Butler's fieldhouse, "we're down by seven points. It's crunch time and we gotta play like never before."

"We ain't ready to lose," Clarence said, wiping off his goggles.

"Yeah, we gonna make it to the 'Sweet Sixteen'," Reggie added. "Let's play hard, guys!"

"D is the key," LaMont told the Patriots as they walked onto the floor for the final quarter.

Brian felt more exhausted than he'd ever felt during a game. But then he looked up at the scoreboard at one end of the court and was determined to win the game.

North inbounded the ball to Alex Hall, who passed it to Bull Howard in the foul lane. The six-five forward turned and swished a jumper over Clarence's long arms.

It was a bad start for the Patriots.

The score was now Pyle 51 and Jefferson 42.

"Come on, guys, it's now or never," Terry said as he dribbled downcourt on offense.

Brian and the other big players for the Patriots suddenly came to life.

Reggie, back in the game, whipped a pass to LaMont, who up-faked with the ball and drove to the hoop against Bull Howard. Carrington switched over to guard LaMont, leaving Brian free for a pass. LaMont zipped a behind-the-back pass to Brian, who dunked the ball.

The Jefferson fans rose and cheered, then stayed on their feet. The score was now Pyle 51, the Patriots 44.

The teams traded baskets for three minutes, with Carrington scoring on tip-ins and Brian on jump shots.

With three minutes to play, and the score Pyle 61 and Jefferson 58, Terry dribbled across mid-court. The Patriots needed a hoop. But Marty

LaRue caught Terry off guard and stole the ball—then dribbled it off his own foot.

The ball rolled across the floor. Brian and Bull Howard dived for it, sliding and skinning their knees.

Brian reached the ball first and slapped it to Reggie, who turned and whipped a pass to Clarence under the basket. Reed leaped and slam-dunked the ball, and Jefferson trailed by only one point, 61–60.

The Butler fieldhouse erupted with loud cheers.

After the teams traded lay-ups, one by Hall for Pyle and a reverse lay-up by LaMont for the Patriots, only ninety seconds remained in the game. The Packers had the ball.

With the score Pyle 63 and Jefferson 62, Marty LaRue passed the ball to Carrington near the basket. The six-six center turned, pump-faked twice, then shot a jumper. Brian timed his leap, stretched, and blocked the shot.

Reggie grabbed the loose ball, then raced down-court and passed it to LaMont, who made a lay-up.

The Patriots' fans jumped and went wild in the bleachers. They looked like a sea of red-white-and-blue pom-poms.

The score now was Jefferson 64 and Pyle 63, and it was the Patriots' first lead of the game.

Forty-five seconds were left to play, and Pyle called a time-out. Everybody was standing in the bleachers.

"Okay, look for a pass to Carrington inside," Coach Ford told the Patriots. Brian could barely hear him above the music and cheers in the fieldhouse. "Don't foul."

"They might pass to Hall first," Coach Williams

added, "but then watch for a pick by Howard, and a cut by Carrington."

The teams returned to the court, and Howard passed the ball to Hall, who dribbled downcourt.

Thirty-five seconds were left to play.

Hall and LaRue passed the ball between them at the top of the key. Brian, LaMont, and Clarence guarded closely under the basket and waited for Carrington to make his move.

With fifteen seconds left in the game, Carrington cut around Bull Howard's pick and caught a pass from Hall.

The fans screamed as Carrington jumped and shot.

Brian fought around the muscular Howard, leaped toward Carrington, but missed the blocked shot.

The ball banked off the backboard and through the basket. With ten seconds left, Pyle now led 65–64.

Clarence passed the ball inbounds to Terry, but Marty LaRue was guarding him closely. Terry missed the pass and the ball started to bounce out of bounds.

"Get the ball!" LaMont shouted.

Brian, starting to run downcourt for a last-second shot, changed direction and ran after the ball. He dived, slid five feet across the floor, and just before the ball rolled off the court, batted it into Reggie's hands.

Seven seconds were left to play, and Brian shot to his feet and raced downcourt behind Reggie.

With four seconds to play, Reggie was double-teamed by Hall and LaRue in the foul lane and passed the ball to Brian at the top of the key.

The scoreboard clock ticked away the seconds—0:03, 0:02. Brian drove to the basket and launched a running jump shot from ten feet away. Wilbur Carrington leaped and tried to block the shot, but slapped Brian on the arm. The shot missed.

The final buzzer sounded and the happy Pyle fans thought the game was over. They rushed onto the court to celebrate the victory, but the refs blew their whistles and told everybody that Brian had been fouled.

No time was left on the clock. Pyle led 65–64, and Brian was going to shoot two free throws.

The Butler fieldhouse became alive with cheers, half for Brian and half against him. With the foul lane cleared of players from both teams, Brian stepped to the free-throw line. Reggie stepped quickly over to him.

"You make one and it's overtime," Reggie shouted in Brian's ear.

"If I make two, we win," Brian said, smiling. But his stomach felt like a bag of snakes was rolling around inside.

"Two shots," the ref told Brian, handing him the ball.

The Pyle fans shouted and tried to distract Brian.

He bounced the ball twice, took a deep breath, and shot the first free throw. The ball swished through the net.

"All right!" the Patriots' subs shouted.

"Yeah, at least we'll play overtime," Tony yelled.

"One more shot," the ref said, handing the ball to Brian again.

The noise from the Pyle fans was almost deafening as they tried to make Brian miss.

Again he bounced the ball twice, took a deep breath, and shot the ball.

Suddenly, the fieldhouse was deathly silent.

The ball struck the front of the rim, bounced off the back of the rim, and rolled into the hoop.

The Jefferson fans erupted with a loud cheer, then raced onto the court and raised Brian to their shoulders.

The Patriots had won the regional championship by a final score of 66–65!

"Way to go, homeboy!" LaMont shouted, trying to reach up to Brian, who was riding atop the fans' shoulders.

Brian smiled and raised his fists in victory as the rest of the team cheered.

The Jefferson Patriots play against their arch enemies Gary Tech for the State Championships in . . .

PRESSURE PLAY